Dear Diary,

It's happened at last. Darcy Taylor has come home. I always believed she would, despite the glamour and riches of her modeling career. She and Mitchell belong together. I hope they see it before it's too late.

I think I hear the baby crying, so I must go. But one last thing, Dear Diary. Please let me be wise enough to help my family through these troubling times. Help me show Mitch that he deserves to love again. That he'll be a wonderful husband and father. That he wasn't responsible for Angela's death. . .

Dear Reader,

There's never a dull moment at Maitland Maternity! This unique and now world-renowned clinic was founded twenty-five years ago by Megan Maitland, widow of William Maitland, of the prominent Austin, Texas, Maitlands. Megan is also matriarch of an impressive family of seven children, many of whom are active participants in the everyday miracles that bring children into the world.

When our series began, the family was stunned by the unexpected arrival of an unidentified baby at the clinic— unidentified, except for the claim that the child is a Maitland. Who are the parents of this child? Is the claim legitimate? Will the media's tenacious grip on this news damage the clinic's reputation? Suddenly rumors and counterclaims abound. Women claiming to be the child's mother are materializing out of the woodwork! How will Megan get at the truth? And how will the media circus affect the lives and loves of the Maitland children—Abby, the head of gynecology, Ellie, the hospital administrator, her twin sister, Beth, who runs the day-care center, Mitchell, the fertility specialist, R.J., the vice president of operations, even Anna, who has nothing to do with the clinic, and Jake, the black sheep of the family?

Please join us each month over the next year as the mystery of the Maitland baby unravels, bit by enticing bit, and book by captivating book!

Marsha Zinberg,
Senior Editor and Editorial Coordinator, Special Projects

KAREN HUGHES

Formula: Father

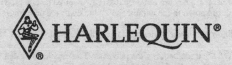

HARLEQUIN®

TORONTO • NEW YORK • LONDON
AMSTERDAM • PARIS • SYDNEY • HAMBURG
STOCKHOLM • ATHENS • TOKYO • MILAN • MADRID
PRAGUE • WARSAW • BUDAPEST • AUCKLAND

HARLEQUIN BOOKS
225 Duncan Mill Road, Don Mills,
Ontario, Canada M3B 3K9

ISBN 0-373-65068-X

FORMULA: FATHER

Copyright © 2000 by Harlequin Books S.A.

Karen Hughes is acknowledged as the author of this work.

Visit us at www.eHarlequin.com

Printed in U.S.A.

Karen Hughes enjoys writing about men and women who want to commit to each other, share dreams and grow old together. She believes romance lives in everyday life and thinks there is a hero inside every man—he just needs the right woman to bring out his best qualities. Wide-open spaces call to Karen, yet she also likes the bustle and convenience of city life. Experience has taught her that true love can be found anywhere.

CHAPTER ONE

DARCY TAYLOR pulled the brim of her baseball cap down, so far, in fact, that the blue bill touched the top of her sunglasses. She wanted to stand outside a little longer, to really drink in the sight of Austin's Maitland Maternity Clinic.

Mayfair Avenue had changed in the years Darcy had been away, but the feel of the street was the same. Or perhaps it was her nostalgic mood playing tricks on her.

She hadn't felt misty a few days ago when she'd stopped by the clinic, but then a few days ago she didn't have an appointment with Mitchell Maitland. Much to her surprise, she'd awakened this morning with a sense of excitement and fear. To see him again...

They had been inseparable. She remembered how she and Mitch had gotten in so much trouble the year they'd set off the firecrackers right underneath the window of the nursery. And there was no way she'd ever forget the day Mitch had kissed her, her very first kiss. Her gaze went to the spot, behind the big oak.

Was it possible? Could it still be...

She crossed the drive quickly, looking over her shoulder to make sure no one was around. When she got to the towering tree, she hesitated, wondering if it would be better not to know. Curiosity won. She circled the massive trunk and searched the bark.

There. Oh, heavens, it was still there. A crudely etched heart. Inside, a simple but heartfelt message: DT+MM FOREVER.

Darcy closed her eyes. She hadn't known then that forever would be one year and two months.

She turned away, angry at herself for being such a sentimental sap. She'd been a kid when she'd used her mother's good steak knife to make her mark on the tree. She wasn't a kid anymore. And now she needed her old friend for the most important thing she'd ever done.

Leaving the tree and her past behind, she headed for the front door and stepped inside. After signing in, she made her way to the main waiting area. The lovely soft pastel walls were as comfy as the couches and chairs chosen specifically for the ease with which very pregnant ladies could sit down on them and stand up again. Three such women sat there, one reading a romance novel, which she perched on her belly, one filing her nails and the third, who didn't look very pregnant, thumbing through last month's issue of *Vogue*.

The receptionist, a youngish woman with gorgeous long hair, smiled. "May I help you?"

"I have an appointment with Mitchell Maitland."

"And you are?"

Darcy took off her glasses and tucked them in her purse. "Darcy Taylor," she said, keeping her voice low so only the receptionist could hear.

The receptionist, who looked to be around the same

age as Darcy, blinked in surprise, then turned to the woman holding the *Vogue*. There, on the cover, was Darcy Taylor, wearing a new Gautier, her hair piled extravagantly on top of her head, her makeup exaggerated and perfected with airbrushing and computer manipulation.

"I'll call Dr. Maitland, Ms. Taylor."

Darcy smiled. "Thank you." She didn't sit down. It was better to stand and wait. Not just because she didn't want to be recognized, but because the moment the receptionist picked up the phone, Darcy's heart started pounding in her chest. She felt her pulse throb and her chest tighten. Her face felt cold, and so did her hands.

She realized right then that she'd made a terrible mistake. What had she been thinking? Of all the doctors in the world, why on earth had she picked him? He might have a reputation for being the best in his field, but surely there were other terrifically competent doctors she could have chosen. Doctors who hadn't kissed her in fourth grade. Doctors who hadn't broken her heart.

"He'll be right down, Ms. Taylor."

Darcy nodded, suddenly unable to speak, her mouth had gone so dry. She grabbed a mint from the desk and got the wrapper off a millisecond before she shoved the candy in her mouth. A moment later, she was able to concentrate on her breathing. On calming herself using techniques she'd learned in front of the camera.

He was an old friend, that's all. Someone she'd known once upon a time. Of course he was the logical

choice to help her. Why not? He'd probably forgotten
all about how she'd left. Why wouldn't he?

Many bridges had been crossed since those long-
ago school days. He'd gone on to fulfill his dream of
becoming a doctor. She'd gone on to fulfill her
mother's dream of becoming a model.

And now, with almost scary synchronicity, she'd
come home to fulfill her own dream. To do the one
thing she wanted most in the world.

She was going to have a child.

Her hand went to her stomach, and she tried to
imagine a life inside her, but her imagination wasn't
good enough. What she could picture was her belly
growing, her body changing. Scary stuff. But not as
scary as a future without a baby.

The muted ding of an elevator made her look up.
The doors hissed open and there, in a white coat that
came down to his knees, dark blue jeans and a white
shirt with a Garfield necktie, stood Mitchell Maitland.

She knew him instantly, even though she hadn't
seen him in years. He had the same unruly dark hair.
The same inquisitive green eyes. The same Maitland
nose. But he'd developed a few things since she'd
seen him last, like those wide shoulders and all that
height—he'd been shorter than she was when she'd
left. Now he stood several inches above her six feet.

Her gaze moved down his body, seeing everything,
every detail. His long, lean legs. The beeper at his
belt. The stethoscope tucked into his coat pocket.

When she reached his tennis shoes, she smiled.
He'd worn tennis shoes to everything from gym class
to church.

"Hey, Taylor," he said, his voice soft, barely above a whisper.

She raised her eyes as he approached. "Hey, Maitland," she said, the old greeting soothing her fears.

"I didn't believe it," he said. "I figured it was some other Darcy Taylor."

"I came by to see Beth but I told her not to mention it. You look great by the way," she said, meaning it.

It was Mitchell's turn to give her the once-over. His gaze traveled over her khaki jumper, down to her woven sandals, then up again. It shouldn't have bothered her in the least. God knows, she'd been looked at enough in her life. But she couldn't remember wanting anyone's approval as fiercely as she wanted his.

He smiled. His crooked grin did something to her insides, made her wish she could turn back time. "You're still the prettiest girl I ever knew."

She took three steps, right into his arms. Into a hug so tight it was a little hard to breathe. She didn't care. For the first time in years, she felt safe. She'd been a fool not to call him before. She could have had years of incredible hugs, years of a friendship that had nothing to do with her looks or her money or the covers of magazines.

His hand moved down her back, pressing her closer, making her aware that this wasn't the same boy she'd known all those years ago. Her eyes fluttered closed as she leaned against the man he was now. The hundred questions that had been on the tip of her tongue seconds ago seemed unimportant. She was home. Back in a world that had brought her more pain and more joy than any she'd experienced since. And most of that joy had been centered around Mitchell Maitland.

When he finally pulled back she met his gaze. Many things had changed in the years she'd been away, but the kindness, the curiosity, the warmth in those green eyes hadn't.

"Shall we go upstairs?"

She nodded.

Mitch turned to lead her to his office, then glanced at Elaine behind the receptionist's desk. Her mouth hung open as she stared blatantly. He knew it wasn't because Darcy was a celebrity—too many celebrities had walked through these doors to rattle Elaine's cage. Her bewilderment came from the fact that Darcy Taylor had hugged *him*. Stodgy, practical, stick-in-the-mud Doc Maitland. He had to admit he enjoyed the look of shock on her face. It felt good to surprise someone for a change.

But then his gaze went to Darcy, and Elaine was instantly forgotten. Darcy took up every bit of his attention. Just getting used to the idea that she was really here was proving quite a task.

He led her to the elevator, and as they waited, he tried twice to ask her questions, only to get flustered each time. There were too many questions, that was the problem. Questions he'd rehearsed a hundred times before, just in case he ever ran into her again.

"Mitch?"

"Yes?"

"I think you have to press the button if we actually want the elevator to come."

He felt heat rush to his cheeks as he leaned over

to press the up button. It occurred to him that the last time he'd blushed, he'd been fifteen years old. Darcy had tripped on a piece of wood on the high school football field, and when she'd fallen, her dress had flown up, revealing a pair of tiny pink lacy underpants. He'd had an immediate, embarrassing, nearly life-threatening erection, and instead of helping her to her feet, he'd run as fast as he could to the boys' locker room.

She hadn't spoken to him for two days, for which he'd been grateful, since he seemed unable to control himself when he got anywhere near her. God, he'd wanted her. Was there ever again such an acute need as that of a fifteen-year-old boy for his first love?

How he'd loved her. More than school, more than his family, more than life itself. And when she left him, it very nearly killed him.

The elevator doors opened, and he touched the small of Darcy's back to usher her inside. He felt a slight quiver under his hand. And then she turned to face the front, and he wasn't quite sure his perception had been accurate.

He remembered to press the button to the second floor, and on the ride up, he wondered how much she knew. His sister Beth and Darcy had kept in touch over the years, although infrequently. Had Beth told her about Angela? About the child? Did Darcy know about the scandals that had rocked the Maitlands? No, probably not. If she had, he doubted she would have come here.

Which led him to the big question—why had she come here? Was it personal? Professional?

The elevator stopped, and he felt tempted to touch

her again, but he held back. Until he found out what was going on, he had to assume that she was a patient and act accordingly.

Darcy walked with him, keeping up with his long stride easily. As they passed a meal cart in the hallway, she moved very close and her scent hit him, soft, evocative, slightly sweet. He found himself reacting to the incredibly feminine fragrance. Or maybe it was just the nearness of her that made his pulse race.

They finally got to his office, and he held the door open for her. As she passed him, he took a deep breath. He wanted to remember the scent. It seemed important.

Darcy didn't sit down right away. She went to his degrees on the wall. Bachelor of Science. Medical Degree. Phi Beta Kappa key. The most important parts of his life were on that wall, including a picture of his family. There was one notable exception: the woman turning to look at him.

"You did it, Maitland."

He smiled at the familiar address. "Yeah, I did, Taylor."

She smiled, too, and he felt his chest tighten. "I've thought about you."

"Oh?"

"I wondered if there was someone at college. You know...." She shook her head slowly. "Someone who challenged you like I did?"

"Challenged? Are you kidding?"

"Have we forgotten so soon?" She took a step toward him, her grin growing more devilish by the second. "Who was it that got the top score on the biology final?"

"Yeah, but who was it that aced the chem final?"

"I still think you cheated."

"Ha."

She met his gaze, and her smile faded. "Ha," she whispered, but he had the feeling the gibe wasn't meant for him.

"You've done pretty well for yourself," he said, wanting to bring back the fire in her eyes.

"Yeah, yeah." Her fingers played over his medical books, and he felt a little surprised that her nails were polished. Which was idiotic. The woman was a fashion model, one of the most famous in the world. Of course she'd have her fingernails polished. She wasn't the kid who espoused the idea that makeup was a plot to keep women subservient and that high heels were a medieval torture device. He wondered if she'd ever really been that kid.

"So what brings you home, Darcy?" He cleared his throat, surprised at how gruff he'd sounded.

She didn't answer him right away. She looked around the room once more, then at him. "It is home, isn't it?"

"I heard you live in New York now."

"Not anymore. I sold my apartment."

"Oh?"

"I bought a house. A great big beautiful house."

"In Manhattan?"

Her smile came back, and it was easy to see why she'd made it to the top of her rarefied world. Her eyes lit up, and the face that had launched a thousand magazines looked luminous and so beautiful it seemed impossible. He rarely noticed the details of a woman's appearance, but with her, he couldn't help it. Her skin looked softer and smoother than any child's. Her eyes, doe-shaped and mysterious, chocolate brown with thick, dark lashes, made him think of Audrey Hepburn. But it was her mouth that had captured the attention of the entire male population. Her lips, which she'd hated as a girl, were her trademark. Almost too generous, her smile suggested much more than a demure kiss. It was sexy and sweet, both at the same time. And then there was something more…something he couldn't identify, even though he'd given it a great deal of thought.

She'd been a beautiful girl, but she'd blossomed into an exquisite woman. A woman who could have any man she wanted. The rich, the famous, the infamous. All she had to do was crook her little finger, and they'd lie down before her. The tabloids had chronicled her love affairs in terrible detail. It was his private masochism that made him keep reading the damn things, even when each word hurt like hell.

She tilted her head to the side, and her hair, as dark and luxurious as mink, fell over her shoulder. "What is that look for?"

"What look?"

"You know what I'm talking about. Come on, Maitland. It's me. The science nerd from fifth grade. The one who helped you get back at Craig Thomas for stealing your homework. Remember?"

"Of course, I remember." He stepped behind his desk, needing the distance and the furniture between them. "But a lot has changed since fifth grade, huh?"

"Maybe not too much? At least I hope not too much. I liked us back then." Her statement and the look in her eyes were enigmatic, and before he could even venture a guess as to what she meant, she moved to the wall of diplomas. "I hear you're *the man* when it comes to fertility."

He laughed as he sat down. "You make it sound like I'm the one doing the fertilizing."

She smiled, too, and for a moment, it was as if they were in high school again. But the feeling left him as quickly as it had come.

"Why did you choose this?" She nodded toward his diplomas, then turned to him again. Her gaze held no humor, just intense curiosity.

"I was going to be a surgeon at first, which was more out of rebellion than a love for surgery. But then I did a rotation in reproductive obstetrics, and everything changed. I figured I could make a difference here at the clinic. And there you have it."

"I have a feeling that was the Cliff Notes version."

"I didn't want to bore you silly."

She sat across from him and leaned forward so her elbows were on the edge of his desk. "Maybe someday you'll tell me the whole story."

He didn't answer her. It didn't seem likely that their paths would cross again. He still wasn't sure why she'd come today.

"Mitch?"

"Yes?"

"Tell me about this artificial insemination. I mean, what it takes."

His curiosity made him speechless for a moment. Was this for her? Was she—

Her right brow rose slightly, and he set his curiosity aside. But as he explained the different methods of insemination, the ovulation kit, the fact that most

pregnancies occur in the first four cycles of therapy
and all the other basics, he couldn't look at her. The
only reason he got through the entire spiel was that
he'd done it hundreds of times before.

When he came to the end of the talk, he met her
gaze, and once more he was reminded of sitting next
to Darcy in algebra, when Mr. Green was explaining
a new concept to the class.

Mitch's grasp of the subject always suffered because he'd end up watching Darcy. No one listened
the way she did. She would lean forward, like now.
Her eyes widened, and when she had her moment of
comprehension—that great aha!—she blinked rapidly
for several seconds. If she didn't understand something, she nibbled on her lower lip.

He'd dreamed about that.

She sat back in the suede wing chair, sighed, and
as if she'd read his thoughts, nibbled on her lower
lip. He forced his gaze away from her mouth. ''You
have questions?''

She nodded. ''The donors,'' she said, her voice a
little timid. ''How does the woman select which
sperm...''

''Assuming it's not going to be the husband's?''

''Yeah. Assuming that.''

''We have a sperm bank here, on the premises.
Each donor is screened very carefully, and we keep
up-to-date profiles on each one.''

''Wow,'' she said, more to herself than him.

''Darcy?''

''Hmm?''

''You want to tell me what this is about?''

She nibbled a little more on that lucky lower lip,

then she took a deep breath. "I've quit modeling. For good. I bought the Kendrick place. In fact, escrow closed this morning. I'm not married, and I don't think I ever will be. I've come back to Austin to have a baby. And I want you to help me."

CHAPTER TWO

DARCY HELD HER BREATH as she watched Mitch go into shock. She wished she knew for sure which tidbit had made him pale. That she was giving up modeling? No. Mitch wouldn't care about that. He'd never been particularly impressed with celebrities or fashion.

That she'd bought the Kendricks' house? They'd played on the great expanse of lawn that was Marjorie and Bob Kendrick's front yard so often, it was like their personal playground, right around the corner from the Maitland house. Darcy had told Mitch that one day she would live there. He hadn't believed her. Frankly, she hadn't believed it, either.

Who was she kidding? The shock had nothing to do with careers or houses. It had everything to do with babies.

Mitch came out of his stupor with a jolt, then coughed to cover his lapse. He opened his mouth, shut it, opened it again, then shook his head as he shut it once more.

"Surprise," she said, trying to lighten the mood.

"To say the least." His voice sounded a bit funny, but at least words had come out this time.

"So, can you help me?"

"Can I? Yes. Should I? I have no idea."

"Why?"

He blinked at her as if she'd missed something incredibly obvious. "Because I— You and I— Because we—"

She grinned. It had always been fun to make Mitch sputter. She'd found that out in sixth grade and had used the knowledge to torment him on a regular basis.

"What are you smiling about?"

"It's good to see you, Maitland."

His shoulders relaxed visibly. "It's good to see you, too. I think."

"Hey, you remember the time capsule?"

His brows furrowed for a moment, and then it came to him; she could see it in his face. "God, I haven't thought of that in years."

"I found it."

"No."

She nodded. "Right where we left it."

"What's in it?"

"I don't know. I figured we'd better open it together."

He leaned back in his chair. "I'll be damned. We buried that…when?"

"Nineteen seventy-seven. September. Right before school started."

"Right." He nodded. "We'd read that book."

"Yeah."

For several minutes, he didn't speak. He'd locked his gaze on a stack of folders on his desk, but she didn't think he was really seeing them. Instead, he was looking at the past, just as she had the moment her shovel had hit the tin lunch box buried under the juniper bushes at the Kendricks' house.

She wondered how long it would take for it to become the Taylor house. Certainly all the people she'd grown up with wouldn't be able to call it that. But her daughter's friends... Or her son's. She wasn't picky.

Mitch caught her eye as he leaned forward again. "What does your mother have to say about this, uh, plan?"

"I guess you haven't heard. My mother died eight months ago."

Again, she'd managed to shock him. "What? I would have heard."

Darcy shook her head. "She was in a nursing home in New York. She'd been sick for a long time."

"I'm sorry."

"Yeah, me, too."

"So it's just you, now, huh?"

Darcy nodded. It was just her now, but not for long. Not if she could help it. Not if Mitch would cooperate. He looked as if he wanted to ask her something. Something awkward, if the doodles on his desk blotter were any indication. "Go on," she said.

"Pardon?"

"Go on and ask me whatever it is. It's all right."

He grinned his acknowledgment at being caught. "I was just wondering.... Is there a donor?"

"No. There isn't."

"What about that veterinarian?"

"You knew about that?"

He nodded, somewhat guiltily. "It was kind of hard to miss."

"Swell. I just love having my personal tragedies broadcast on national news. But no. We're not together anymore. We got divorced almost two years ago.''

''I'm sorry.''

''Don't be. It's much better this way.''

''What— Never mind.''

''What happened is that he was more interested in using my connections to make himself a movie star than he was in being my husband.''

''Ouch.''

''Damn straight, ouch. But one good thing came out of it. This decision.''

Mitch nodded. ''I understand. But I'm still not sure I'm the guy to help you.''

''Why not? And don't stutter around it. Just say what you're thinking.''

''Same old Taylor.''

''Same old Maitland.''

His expression turned serious. ''Darcy, this isn't going to be easy. There's only a twenty-five-percent chance that it's going to work. Even if we do everything right.''

''I understand.''

''No, I'm not sure you do. We'll be a team, you and I. I'll have to know very personal things. Like when you're ovulating. And I'll be the one examining you.''

She bit her lip to hide her smile. ''You're embarrassed.''

''Don't be ridiculous. I'm thinking about you.''

''No, you're not. I can read you like a book. You're thinking how weird it's going to be if I'm your patient.''

''Aren't you?''

She nodded. "Sure. It's going to be weird, but only for a little while. Then you'll get involved in the work, and I'll be just another patient."

"You'll never be just another patient."

"I'm going to take that as a compliment."

"I'm not so sure about that, either."

"Come on, Maitland. This is the scariest thing I've ever done. I'm leaving everything I know behind me and starting a completely new life. It would mean a lot to me to have a friend there to help. I'll go to a stranger if you want me to, but I've thought long and hard about this. I trust you more than I've ever trusted another human being. Despite…" She didn't want to go there. Not now. "We have a lot of history together. We're the brain patrol, remember? Who else is going to care more?"

He stared at her for a long while, his face expressionless. All she could do was wait, prepared for either answer. If it was yes, she'd have some work ahead of her. Not with the baby, but with Mitch. They'd need to talk about what had happened all those years ago. Clear the air. If he said no, then she'd leave him be. She'd find a good doctor and go on with her life. She'd still have Beth's friendship to bolster her. And perhaps, in time, she and Mitch would be able to talk. She sure didn't want to open that time capsule by herself.

"Can you give me some time?" he asked finally. "There's a lot to consider."

"Sure. Of course. Take all the time you need. As long as it's in the next few days."

"Gee, how generous."

"Not to get too personal or anything, but remember that ovulation we talked about?"

He held up his hand to stop her. "I get it."

"Good. Oh, and Mitch?"

"Yeah?"

"Can you keep this under your hat? I don't want the press getting wind of any of this."

"You know I'd never say a word."

She nodded. "Yes, I do know that." She stood, took a step toward the door, then turned to him. "I was wondering if you had time to give me a little tour of the place before I go?"

He shook his head. "Sorry, I've got a patient waiting. But maybe tomorrow...."

"No, it's okay. Really."

"Hold on a sec." He picked up his phone and hit two numbers. A few seconds passed, then he asked his sister Abby if she could take Darcy around.

Darcy remembered Abby from school. She'd been two years behind Mitch and her. Abby was a great choice to show her around. Even as a girl, Abby had had her finger on the pulse of the world. Darcy had never been terribly close to her, but they'd been friendly.

Mitch hung up the phone. "She'll be up in a minute. I would have asked Beth, but I know she's got a meeting this morning."

"It'll be good to see Abby again."

"I just wish I was free."

"Don't worry about it, Maitland. We'll talk. Real soon."

He got up and walked around the desk. She could tell he wanted to put his arm around her, but he wasn't sure if he should. She helped him out by hugging him first. A first-class major squeeze. It was impossible not to close her eyes when she felt his hands on her back. When he pulled her close. When she took a deep breath of his masculine scent.

If things had been different…

MITCH DIDN'T CALL IN his next patient right away. He took a moment, leaned back in his chair and closed his eyes. It was important not to go crazy about this. What had happened to them was ancient history. Nothing to get all worked up about.

So why was his stomach churning? Why did he feel this crushing weight of disappointment?

Because he'd loved her, that's why. He'd been young, yes, and he'd been naive, but the fact was he'd loved her, and he thought she loved him back. Now, once and for all, he knew he'd been mistaken. Darcy hadn't loved him. If she had, she never would have asked him to be her doctor. Her emotions would have been too vulnerable. Yes, it had been years, but time could never diminish the pain of a first love gone wrong.

What shook him up most, however, was the awful realization that after all this time, even after Angela, he'd obviously still harbored hope that someday Darcy would come back. That she'd be his.

He was a first-class fool.

Darcy had left him without a second thought and gone on to a life he could hardly imagine. Of course she hadn't thought about the kid who'd helped her with her science project. She was too busy with movie stars and politicians. Traveling all over the world. Smiling for the camera and her adoring public.

It was pure sentiment that had brought her here today. Some warm, fuzzy feeling about their childhood antics.

But what he was feeling was neither warm nor fuzzy. It hurt. It hurt as if she'd left him yesterday. It hurt because a dream had died. A dream he hadn't even realized he'd had.

He couldn't help her. He'd give her a referral, and that would be the end of it. Maybe it was a blessing. Maybe knowing the truth would set him free. He hadn't been serious about a woman since Angela.

He looked at the clock, and that got him up and moving, but it didn't stop his feverish thoughts. Why, of all the people in the world, did Darcy Taylor want artificial insemination? She could have any man she wanted. The best and the brightest would line up to father her child. But she'd asked about the donors at the clinic.

And why, at the peak of her career, had she quit? Something wasn't right. It didn't add up.

He went to examination room four and plucked the chart from the wall pocket. The minute he saw the name of his patient, he focused completely on her. Well, almost completely. Just before he knocked on the door, he closed his eyes and took a calming breath. An earthquake had hit Austin, and the epicenter was right here inside him. The world that had been steady and predictable this morning had been shaken so hard, he couldn't get a foothold.

Darcy Taylor had come back.

DARCY SIPPED her coffee as she looked around the diner. It was a cheery place, with a regular clientele. She remembered the owner, Shelby Lord, as a spunky little girl with red hair, a friend of Beth and Ellie's. She had obviously done well for herself with the restaurant. Darcy took another drink of the terrific coffee, then picked up her menu. As she tried to decide between the garden salad and a hot fudge sundae, Abby slipped into the seat across from her.

"The food here is great," she said, picking up a menu. "Shelby will be surprised to see you." Abby nodded toward the counter where a pretty blonde was serving a man in a business suit. "That's Sara. What that poor thing has gone through..." Abby shook her head, then looked at the menu.

"Well?"

The dark-haired doctor, who looked so much like Mitchell only softer and prettier, seemed surprised at her tone. "What?"

"Well, come on. Spill."

"Oh," Abby said, glancing toward the counter. "It's been a three-ring circus around here lately, I swear. I don't know if you've read anything about what's been happening."

"I know about the baby left on your back steps. Have you figured out who the father is?"

"Well," she said, leaning closer and lowering her voice, "that's a story all its own. After we found the baby, this woman, Tanya Lane, showed up with that nightmare from *Tattle Today TV*, Chelsea Markum—"

"I've met her before. Once she gets wind of a story, she never backs off."

"I'll say. Anyway, Tanya claimed the baby was hers and that my brother R.J. was the father."

"R.J.? Are you kidding? He's the straightest person I've ever met."

Abby nodded. "So you can imagine how that freaked him out. Especially when Tanya said that he'd deserted her when he found out she was pregnant!"

"This is positively surreal!"

"Oh, there's more. We lost a lot of patients over that. And I can't tell you how many regrets we got at first for the twenty-fifth-anniversary party. Which you're invited to, by the way."

"When is it?"

"A week and a half."

"Okay, go on."

"*Tattle Today* must have had some real suspicions about Tanya, though, because they put up fifty thousand dollars for an exclusive interview with whoever proved to be the real mother. Of course, busloads of women showed up, each one claiming the baby, and thanks to an article in the tabloids, every one of them swore Jake was the father."

"My God. Jake. Is he still Mr. Mystery?"

"That's an understatement. Jake hadn't been home for five years, so they figured he couldn't defend himself. But it didn't do them any good. None of them knew that there was a birthmark on the baby."

"A birthmark?"

Abby nodded. "Right above his belly button."

"So Jake was off the hook?"

"Not quite. He came home after Mother called him, with a very pregnant woman in tow."

"*Another* mystery baby?"

"Imagine our delight." Abby sighed.

Darcy was having trouble assimilating all this in one sitting. It must have been a madhouse. "So what happened?"

Abby took a drink of water and signaled the waitress. After she ordered a piece of pie, Darcy ordered the sundae. When they were alone once more, Darcy looked at the menu again, then tried to get the waitress back.

"What's wrong?" Abby asked.

"I don't know if I can do it."

"Do what?"

"Eat a hot fudge sundae."

"Why not?"

Darcy felt a tug of emotion in her chest and swallowed a little lump in her throat. "I've been a slave to food for sixteen years. Every mouthful mattered. Calories were the enemy, and I could never let my guard down."

"That must have been awful."

"You have no idea. I always felt like I was being punished. But no more. I'm not going to do that to myself, not even for one meal. I'm going to eat like a normal person. If I can figure out what normal people eat."

"We eat hot fudge," Abby said, her smile understanding and warm, making Darcy feel she'd made the right choice coming to Maitland Maternity. "Not every day, but we do eat it."

"The mind fairly boggles."

"If you have any trouble on the dessert front, just call me. I'll do my best to lead the way."

"It's a deal." Darcy put the menu down. "So where were we?"

Abby frowned. Played with a packet of sugar. "Jake came home with his pregnant friend. In the meantime, we had another surprise arrival. Connor O'Hara, my cousin, whom we'd never even met before. It turns out that he's the father of the baby. His girlfriend, Janelle, saw all the hoopla on television, and she came to claim the baby."

"Why did she abandon the baby in the first place? I can't imagine any mother doing that."

"I know. But she said that she and Connor had broken up and then she couldn't find him. She'd lost her job and had no family of her own, so she brought the baby here, knowing Connor was related to us."

"Why didn't she just knock on the front door?"

Abby shrugged. "I'm not sure. I haven't spent much time with her. Or Connor, for that matter." She looked away, and Darcy was surprised to see her cheeks infuse with pink. "I was a little busy."

"Oh?"

She held out her left hand, flashing a beautiful diamond ring.

"You got married?"

She grinned. "I sure did."

"Who is he?"

"His name is Kyle McDermott."

Darcy watched as Abby's mouth softened into a smile of pure contentment. It was so clear she was in love. Radiantly in love. Darcy had to look away.

"He's wonderful," Abby went on. "Stubborn as a mule, but his heart is so good. Darcy, you'll love him. We'll have dinner, okay? Soon."

"I'd like that," Darcy said.

The waitress came by with their desserts, and for a few minutes, all Darcy could do was wallow in the sinful indulgence. But then Abby looked at the time. "I've got a meeting in about fifteen minutes."

"So tell me the rest. I won't sleep tonight if I don't hear it all."

"Okay. So Janelle moves into the guest cottage at Mother's."

Darcy smiled, remembering how she and Mitchell used to sneak into that little house.

"Just until she gets the official birth records, of course. Social Services insisted. Now that she and Connor are engaged, Connor's moved into the cottage with her."

Darcy nodded. "I see."

"But that whole issue was pushed to the back burner when they found the dead woman in Beth's office." Abby stopped to take another bite of cherry pie before going on. "I can't explain it, but even that turned out to be lucky, in a way. She and Ty Redstone..." Abby raised her eyebrows suggestively.

"Really? I thought something was up, but Beth didn't say a word."

"Oops. I'll let her be the one to tell you, then."

"Fair enough," Darcy agreed.

Abby took another bite of pie. "Long story shorter than I'd like to make it is that Mother announced that the baby's mother has come forward but wishes to remain anonymous. After that, all the people who'd sent their regrets changed their minds and accepted the invitation to the gala, which means it's going to be a zoo."

"Oh, dear. I'm not too happy to hear about that."

"Why not?"

"I don't particularly want this Chelsea Markum to know I'm here."

"Oh, yeah. I didn't think about that."

"I'll have to pass on the party. But thanks for asking."

"If you change your mind…"

Darcy nodded. "I know you have to leave in a minute, but you never did tell me about the woman behind the counter."

Abby leaned over again, making sure no one could hear her but Darcy. "She doesn't know who she is. She was evidently in some kind of accident. Lost her memory completely."

"Are you kidding?"

Abby shook her head. "The only thing she knows for sure is that she's a fabulous cook. Shelby told me last night that she's going to ask Sara to be a chef instead of a waitress."

"Wow, amnesia," Darcy said, only half listening to Abby. She couldn't imagine what that would be like.

"I've really got to go, Darcy. I'm sorry."

"No, it's fine. You go. I'm going to stay and finish every bite of this sundae. And don't you dare put that money down. It's my treat. The tour was great, but frankly, the gossip was even better."

"We'll talk more."

"You bet we will."

Darcy waved goodbye, then turned to her ice cream. Now that she was alone, she allowed herself to think about her problems. Mitchell, of course. But also the fact that Maitland Maternity was in the spotlight so often. It seemed hard to believe that so much had hit the family all at once. Maybe she should go to another doctor and not take such a big risk.

Now, if she could only figure out which risk she was so afraid of taking—being discovered by the media or rekindling her...friendship with Mitchell Maitland.

The hot fudge didn't help her solve her problem—but it sure made the worry a lot easier to take.

CHAPTER THREE

THE BABY GURGLED, and Janelle forced herself to laugh. She tickled the baby's tummy as she widened her smile. Then she saw that the damn snooty butler, Harold, had finally left the room and she could relax. But not too much. Anyone could walk in at any second. Megan Maitland was the biggest nuisance, but at least she was convinced that Chase was her grandson and Connor her real son and that she, Janelle, was the nicest, sweetest, most loving daughter-in-law-to-be in the world.

She couldn't put it off any longer. She had to change the baby's diaper. Nothing made her want to gag more. Well, nothing except seeing the self-righteous Maitland family being all lovey-dovey with each other. That was enough to make anyone sick.

All she had to do was keep it up for a little while longer. Just until Petey and she made their money, and then it was adios to Austin, to the Maitlands, to this.... She took off the old diaper and winced at the smell.

She didn't dare do anything less than a thorough job, though. Megan or Harold would check. They always did. Like they didn't trust her or something.

She laughed. Man, her only regret was that she

wouldn't be around to see their faces when they realized what she'd done. How she'd tricked them all.

Ironically, she figured Megan would be the one who could appreciate her work the most. Megan, who was tough as nails behind that angelic facade. Megan, who hadn't gotten where she was by being a Goody Two-shoes. No one made that kind of money by being sweet.

Megan had had to be smarter than the other guy, one step ahead. Just like Janelle. And that's why it was all going to work, pretty as you please. Then she'd live her life in the kind of luxury she deserved. As for Petey... If he behaved, he'd be right there next to her. If he didn't?

Sacrifices had to be made sometimes. God knows, changing diapers should have been sacrifice enough. But if she had to do this alone, so be it.

Petey. So damn good-looking. So malleable. But not exactly the brightest bulb in the chandelier. Actually, it was probably better that he wasn't. Wouldn't want him getting too many ideas of his own.

Finally, the kid was changed. And Megan would be down any second to take the brat to the Maitland day care. Janelle could wait. She'd learned all about waiting.

She picked up the baby and held him to her chest. As she walked around the room, bouncing him gently, a thought occurred to her. What if she didn't leave? What if she stayed right here in Austin. Took Megan Maitland down a few hundred pegs. Took over the mansion!

Wouldn't that be a day. My, my. This would require some thought. Some serious thought.

"YOU'RE STILL HERE!"

Darcy nodded as she walked toward Beth. "I'm on my way out. I just thought I'd stop in and say a quick hello first."

Beth stepped over a pile of Lego, dodged a headless Barbie and maneuvered deftly around a See-n-Spell that mooed for no apparent reason. "Did you and Abby have a nice lunch? I was so sorry to miss out." She embraced Darcy in a fierce hug, then her hands grasped Darcy's upper arms, which she held as she studied her friend's face. "I swear to God, you are more gorgeous than anyone I've ever met."

"Oh, come on."

"I'm not kidding."

Darcy smiled, knowing that Beth meant it as a compliment and not as an opening line to precede a favor.

"You know I'm not lying. You could always tell when I was."

"And you did plenty of it, if my memory serves."

Beth's grin was exactly the same as when she'd been seven years old, and Darcy had been her babysitter. "I was a perfect angel as a child. And I refuse to believe anything different."

Darcy couldn't help but laugh. Beth had always been so cheerful, so excited about life.

"Do you have a minute? I want to hear what Mitchell said when you told him why you were here."

"That won't take long. He said—"

"No, not yet. I'm supposed to be on a break, so why don't I walk you to your car."

"Really?"

She nodded, sending her dark curly hair bobbing down her back. Darcy wanted to tell her what a beautiful woman she'd become, but she decided to wait till their next meeting. She didn't want it to sound as if she were just returning Beth's compliment.

"I'll be one second." Beth scurried to the far side of the day care to speak to an older woman who was helping a little boy fix a toy truck.

Darcy's gaze swept the large, cheerful place until she noticed the garden outside. Lush and green, with all sorts of intriguing plants, it seemed a perfect place to find peace and quiet.

At that thought, a great shriek rang out, and Darcy spun to find a little girl—she looked to be around five—howling like a banshee, her face scrunched up in a mask of pure misery. Darcy rushed over to her, searching for blood or a broken bone at the very least. What she found instead was a baby doll with black marker on its face. Two big dark circles, as if the doll had lost a barroom brawl.

Darcy crouched so she was nearly eye level with the girl, who, she saw, would be extremely pretty if she ever stopped crying. "Honey, are you crying because of your doll?"

The girl sniffed and nodded, which caused a teardrop to fall on Darcy's hand. She completely melted. Then she took the doll and tried to wipe off the black marker, but it didn't help. The shiners were there for keeps. She'd have to try another tack. "What's your name, sweetie?"

After another sniff, the girl mumbled something Darcy didn't catch.

"What is it?"

"Courtney."

"Oh, that's a beautiful name." She held up the doll. "And what's her name?"

"Lizabeth."

"That's a beautiful name, too. But you know what?"

Courtney shook her head, still looking so woeful it broke Darcy's heart.

"She's going to need your help from now on."

"What?"

"Lizabeth. She's very special now, and it will take a very special little girl to care for her properly."

"She's no good anymore. Gilbert ruined her."

"Gilbert didn't ruin her. He gave her a cross to bear. Do you know what that means?"

Again, Courtney shook her head. But at least she'd stopped crying.

"It means that she's different from all the other dolls. Her eyes make her different. Now, most people don't like things that are different. They don't realize how wonderful it is to love someone like Lizabeth."

"Why is it wonderful?"

"Because you know what Lizabeth is really like. You know that behind all this marker, there's a sweet, beautiful doll, right?"

"Uh-huh."

"So when your friends see you treating her as if she were brand-new and perfect, they'll learn to see past the black marker, too."

"Really?"

"Really. And before you know it, Lizabeth will be the most popular doll in the whole day care."

Courtney wiped her face with the back of a perfect

tiny hand. She reached for the battered doll, which Darcy put carefully into her arms. Then, without a goodbye, Courtney headed across the room.

Darcy watched her go to the playhouse and crawl inside, taking the doll with her.

"You're gonna be one heck of a great mother," Beth said.

Darcy looked up at her voice. She'd been so intent on Courtney that she hadn't even realized Beth was standing right behind her.

"You know, we're always looking for good help here."

Darcy smiled as she rose. "No, thanks. With any luck at all I'm going to have a full-time job as a mommy very soon."

"Which brings us back to what Mitchell said."

"In a nutshell, he said he wasn't keen on the idea of being my doctor."

"Which you'd anticipated."

"Yes, but now—" she looked at the playhouse once more "—now I know I need to convince him to take me on."

"Why?"

"Because this is my home. And, like it or not, you guys are the closest thing I've got to family. And I'm going to need all of you to help me with this child."

Beth held open the door for her and they stepped into the hall. "I'll do what I can to help."

"I know you will. And I appreciate that more than you can imagine."

"I've needed the family to stand by me, too. Mitchell will come through. He always does."

They were walking by the elevators when a very tall, very good-looking man approached Beth.

"Excuse me. I'm looking for Megan Maitland."

"And you are?"

"Harrison Smith. I'm here to discuss my daughter's care."

"Is she a patient here?"

"No, but she might turn out to be one. If things check out."

"I'm sure you'll find there's no safer place for your daughter in the world," Beth assured him. "Or better care."

He nodded, but Darcy had the feeling he wasn't convinced.

"Megan Maitland's office is upstairs. There's a receptionist who will call her for you."

"Thank you."

Darcy took a step toward Beth as they watched the man ring for the elevator. They didn't speak again until the doors had closed behind him and the elevator had started moving.

"What a stunner," Beth said.

"How old do you think he was?"

"Forty. Maybe forty-five."

"Did you see those dark blue eyes?"

Beth nodded. "And that thick black hair?"

"God, if Lagerfeld ever got a hold of a man like that," Darcy said. "I can just see him on the cover of *GQ*."

"Until a month or so ago, I know exactly where I would have liked to have seen him," Beth said, leading Darcy toward the front door. "But not anymore.

Harrison Smith might be tall, dark and handsome, but he can't come close to Ty Redstone.''

"Aha. I was wondering when you were going to tell me about him. Abby hinted…"

Beth smiled broadly. "He's the most wonderful man in the whole world. And, oh, Darcy, I can hardly believe it myself, but we're going to be married!''

Darcy was happy for her old friend. Honestly happy. But that didn't stop her heart from aching. From wanting her own eyes to shine with a love so deep and real, everything else in the world faded into the background.

She might not ever find that kind of love for herself, but she could give that kind of love to a child. To her child. But this was no time to be wrapped up in her own angst. Beth was going to be married. Darcy hugged her friend once more. "I want to hear all about him," she said.

"Don't worry, you will.''

"DON'T YOU HAVE an opinion?''

Mitchell focused on his mother, knowing he'd missed the gist of their conversation. The last thing he remembered clearly was telling her about Darcy's sudden appearance. Then he'd gone somewhere else, even though he hadn't left the room. "What was the question again?''

Megan Maitland shook her head, but her smile was sympathetic. "I imagine it's difficult to see her again after all this time.''

He nodded. "But it's also good. I mean, we sure went through a lot together.''

Megan studied him in that way she had, as if she

could see inside him. She'd had that ability even when he'd been a child. He'd never been able to lie to her. She'd always known. "Sometimes," she said, "the one we love first is the hardest to forget."

He jerked in his chair. "Love? Who said anything about love? We were friends. Damn good friends. But it didn't go further than that."

"No? My mistake. Sorry."

Mitch cleared his throat. "So who is this man we're meeting?"

His mother didn't answer, not in words, at least. But her gaze said she wasn't fooled. As much as he hated to admit it, he wasn't fooled, either. Darcy had been his first love. But that had been years ago. A lot had changed since then.

"His name is Harrison Smith. He's here to discuss his daughter's birthing plans." She glanced at the antique clock on her desk. "And he's late."

"Why am I here? Shouldn't he be talking to Abby?"

"I want your take on him. Something seemed a little off when he made his appointment. He wanted to make sure we knew how much money he had and that he was willing to spend it on his daughter."

"Sounds good to me."

"Mitchell," she said, scolding him, but lightly. "With all that's gone on here in the last few months, you don't expect me to ignore a gut feeling, do you?"

"Your gut feeling? No way."

"Thank you. Besides, you know as much about the clinic as anyone, so you'll be able to answer any questions he might have about the medical side of things."

"I'll do my best."

"That's all I expect."

He got up and went to the window. He found what he was looking for in two seconds. The great old tree with their initials carved in the trunk. DT+MM FOR-EVER. Darcy Taylor plus Mitchell Maitland. He'd found it two weeks after she'd disappeared. And for the next five years, he'd wanted to forget that he'd ever seen it. It was a cruel joke by a sadistic universe. He'd been so shy he'd never been able to tell her his true feelings. And he'd certainly never guessed he was anything more than a friend to Darcy. And then to find out they'd wasted all that time. That they could have been so much more, if only they'd told each other the truth.

He'd often wondered if she might not have left if he'd had the nerve to tell her he loved her. The course of their lives would have been different. It could have been everything he ever wanted.

All because he couldn't find the courage to say three little words.

"Mrs. Maitland?" The bright voice came over the intercom. "Mr. Smith is here for his appointment."

"Bring him in, please."

Mitchell found his seat again, prepared for a boring half hour. Then Harrison Smith entered the room, and boring wasn't even in the ballpark.

Something happened between Smith and his mother. It might have been recognition. It definitely was a jolt. His mother never lost her cool, and yet, for a moment, when her hand touched Smith's, she'd grown so pale he was afraid she might pass out. The next second, she was back to her old self. Stately, calm and more charming than any other woman he'd met.

Mitch's gaze shifted to Smith to see if he, too, had felt something odd. But there was nothing to read on his face. The only thing slightly amiss was the way he looked at Megan. He stared, hard, as if memorizing her features.

Then Mitch got it. He almost laughed out loud when he realized what he was doing. Nothing was going on with Harrison Smith and his mother. It was a classic case of transference. What he'd seen in his mother's eyes was his projection of what had happened to him when he saw Darcy. Of course. His old psychology professor would have had a good laugh.

He relaxed into his chair and listened to Megan talk about the clinic. Once she got going, no one could turn her down. Smith sat rapt, completely under her spell. He waited until she'd finished before he started asking questions. Even when Mitch answered, Smith's gaze focused on Megan. That was a little odd. But the questions were all reasonable, if a little obsessive. It was obvious the man was concerned. He wanted to know about the food, the credentials of everyone from the nurses to the anesthesiologist, but mostly he wanted to know the history of the place.

As Megan talked, Mitchell's gaze went to the window again. How remarkable that a moment's decision could change everything. How sad that fear could lock so many doors and chip away at a man's confidence.

Right then and there he decided to take Darcy Taylor as his patient. An unlucky man let fear rule him once. A fool did it twice.

CHAPTER FOUR

MEGAN MAITLAND stared at the photograph of her late husband, William. Such a handsome man. Such a good man. She missed him as if he'd physically been a part of her, and his absence left a hole that would never be filled. Most days, it was a quiet ache, but sometimes, like right now, it hurt like the dickens.

That Harrison Smith. What was it about him that seemed so familiar? He'd sworn they'd never met, but she wasn't quite so sure. There was something....

It was nice to see a man so concerned about his child. His questions had been astute, if a little odd. He'd wanted to know so much about the clinic, the history, the employees. But it spoke well of him that he cared enough to dig for details. What we do for the love of our children...

Her thoughts turned to the baby. To her grandchild. He was so precious. So perfect in every way. Such a miracle in her life.

She'd never admit it to a living soul, but she was glad Janelle was having trouble getting the birth records for the baby. It was selfish, but Megan didn't care. Having Chase in the house had changed everything. The sound of his laughter, the sweet smell of his freshly washed skin, the sense of utter peace and contentment when he slept. If she wasn't so darned old, she'd have another child herself.

Smiling at her foolishness, she turned to her correspondence. The gala was so close, and there was still so much left to do.

Beth had told her this morning that she was determined to convince Darcy to attend. Darcy. Such a beautiful girl. Such a sweet girl.

Memories tumbled on top of one another. Darcy and Mitch, the terrible twosome. They'd been so good for each other. It had been a shame about Darcy's father. His gambling had done so much to hurt her. And Darcy's mother had worked two jobs to keep them afloat. Poor child. Such a hard beginning. But look what she'd accomplished! What was that old saying about the sharpest swords being forged in the hottest fire? In Megan's experience, it was true. Darcy had become a formidable woman.

Now, wouldn't it be lovely if Mitch and Darcy...

Perhaps that was too much to hope for. Life rarely made sense, especially when it came to matters of the heart. But it would be quite something.

Enough daydreaming. Her work wasn't going to finish itself.

MITCH CLIMBED the steps to the second floor of his town house, but instead of going into his bedroom, he detoured into the guest room. It had been ages since he'd been in there, although the maid who came every two weeks kept it spotless.

He wasn't sure what he was looking for until he opened the closet. Until he saw the boxes that hadn't been opened since he'd moved from his family home.

He got the biggest box down and put it on the bed. It wasn't taped shut. On top of the pile of mementos was his old high school sweatshirt, which meant that he had the right box. Below that were trophies. Mostly for science projects and junior achievers, but also for track and field meets, where he'd been a distance runner. He piled the awards on top of the sweatshirt.

There it was. His high school yearbook. He lifted the heavy book, but he didn't open it. Not yet. Instead, he left it on the bed as he repacked the box, then took the book with him and went to his bedroom.

He stared at the yearbook, green with his high school emblem embossed on the cover, while he took off his coat and tie. Once more, he lifted the book and headed downstairs.

It felt as if every step opened a new door in his memory. The smell of the hallways by the chemistry labs. The smooth, cool surface of the staircase handrail. Mr. Johnson's awful toupee.

By the time he reached the first floor, he was awash in the past, swimming through an ocean of moments that had made up his life.

Above everything, coloring everything, was Darcy.

He poured himself a glass of Merlot, then went to the living room and settled in his favorite leather club chair. But still, he didn't open the book. He sipped his wine, ran his hand over the binding, closed his eyes. She had always been there. At the time, he'd believed that would never change, no matter what. She was his reason.

His reason to study so hard. His reason to join the

glee club. His reason to wake up in the morning. And his reason to dream.

And then she was gone. No goodbye. No warning. Just gone.

He opened the yearbook, but he didn't try to find her picture. It wasn't in there. She'd left two months before graduation. One Friday she'd been in the library, sitting across from him as they studied for a French test, then she disappeared.

He could still remember every detail of that Sunday afternoon. Mrs. Taylor opening the door, looking unkempt and uncomfortable. Not letting him inside.

When he asked if Darcy was ready for study group, she'd grown so red in the face that he got scared. And then when she told him that Darcy had gone to New York to be a model, he'd thought she was lying.

But she hadn't lied. Darcy had flown to New York, and for the next sixteen years, he'd watched as she'd become internationally famous on runways and magazines around the world. He'd watched her on television in commercial after commercial. He'd seen her wedding pictures.

What he'd realized that Sunday was that he hadn't known Darcy at all. She'd never mentioned wanting to be a model, not even once. He'd asked himself a million times if she'd given any hint, but it was clear his teenage self-obsession had been so encompassing that if she had, he'd missed it.

He turned to the middle of the yearbook, to an old snapshot pressed between the pages. It had started to fade, but he could still make out the colors of her dress.

That stupid yellow dress. She'd worn it to the science fair, and when they'd won first prize for their project, she'd been so excited she'd hugged him fiercely. His hand had moved to hold her, but the yellow dress had an open back. Tiny straps held it up. His hand had touched her bare skin, and his whole world had changed.

The feel of her had made him dizzy. In that one instant, she was more to him than she'd ever been—infinitely more. Her breasts pressed against his shirt, taking her from friend to obsession in ten seconds. He got unaccountably brave and moved his hand down her back, to the curve of her buttocks, and when he was inches away, she'd flown out of his embrace as abruptly as she'd flown in, and he was left with a little biology lesson of his own.

He'd dashed behind the table to hide his embarrassment, although he was absolutely convinced that the whole school, including Darcy, had seen his predicament.

His gaze went to the picture, and he studied the girl who had changed his world. Even then it was easy to see what she would become. Taller than everyone in the class, slender as a reed even as she started to blossom. Her hair, cropped short and slightly disheveled, worked perfectly as a frame for a face that would captivate millions. Those eyes. So famous now. But back then, those eyes had been filled with mischief. With curiosity and excitement. He'd anchored the most important friendship of his life by seeing acceptance in those eyes.

The thought made him wince. He should be ashamed of himself, putting Darcy's friendship above Angela's. It wasn't true, anyway. His sentiment had gotten the best of him because Darcy had come back. That was all.

He should consider himself lucky. He'd had a great friend in Darcy, and after she'd left, he'd eventually found Angela. Kind and sweet, she'd been his from the moment they met. She was an education major, and he was in his second year of residency. Angela with her soft laugh and flaming red hair. Who would have guessed he'd have so little time with her?

And who would have guessed he'd continue to feel guilty about her, even after all this time. That, too, was part of Darcy's legacy. Because, although he'd have died before admitting it to anyone, he knew that he'd never really loved Angela. Not when they were dating. Not when they were married. Not when she'd gotten pregnant. Not even when she was on her death-bed.

Angela had never been first in his heart. Darcy was already there.

THE PHONE CALL had come early in the morning. A request, the woman said, from Dr. Maitland to come in for some blood tests and to fill out paperwork.

But as she sat on the paper sheet that covered the middle of the examination table, Darcy wondered if she'd jumped to conclusions about what it meant.

Had he decided to take her as a patient? Or was this a pretext to see her, only to refer her to another doctor?

She'd lost her ability to read him. Of course she had, what did she expect? They'd been so young, and their combined life experience wouldn't have filled a chapter in a memoir. The cold truth was that they'd never had more than a friendship, and that had ended the day she got on the plane for New York. It was only her need for roots that had brought her back. Not her need for Mitchell Maitland—except for his expertise.

Last night she'd been restless, and it was more from her thoughts about Mitchell than the noises in the hotel. She'd waffled so much about having him as her doctor, she'd ended up falling asleep from sheer exhaustion.

But before that final lights-out, she'd at least been able to see that her emotional upheaval hadn't been about Mitchell per se, but about what he represented. With him, life had been innocent and enchanting, and the world had held nothing but promise. That's why she wanted her child to be born here. And why she'd gone to Mitch. If he helped her have this baby, she knew beyond a shadow of a doubt that the Maitlands would keep an eye on the child. Just as they'd kept an eye on her when she'd had so much trouble at home.

The question that kept nagging at her was whether she was being fair to them. Maybe she should just come right out and ask.

She heard a soft knock at the door, and she sat up straighter. It was Mitch. Her chest constricted at the sight of him, and she felt as though she couldn't get enough air. She tried to read his decision in his expression, but she got lost somewhere in those dark green eyes.

He had his hand on the door, but he didn't push it closed behind him. His hesitance was mirrored in his gaze. Should he or shouldn't he? Would he be part of her future or her past?

When he exhaled, she realized she'd been holding her breath, too. When he smiled at her, she realized she'd been holding her heart at bay for longer than she cared to remember.

"Thanks for coming in at the last minute," he said, his voice warming her like a blanket.

She nodded, wanting to prod him along, afraid to speak in case it sidetracked him.

He looked at her carefully, and this time his gaze was more clinical. This was Dr. Maitland, the man with the diplomas on the wall, and he was examining her with all the earnestness he'd had as a student.

Please say yes, she prayed. *Say yes, and give my unborn baby the kind of childhood I've always dreamed of.*

He cocked his head. "Darcy?"

"Yes?"

"Know what I thought of this morning?"

"What?"

"Twenty-two, fourteen, twenty-seven."

She grinned, knowing immediately what the numbers meant. "My locker."

He nodded. "That unholy mess you called a locker."

"It had character."

"It had mold."

She laughed. She had her answer. And maybe she had her friend back.

He grinned, too, as he approached her. After he put her chart on the shelf to his right, he took her hands in his. "Are you sure you want me to help you with this inception?"

She nodded.

"You realize I'm going to have to examine you. Often."

"Yeah, I know. Believe me. A few years ago, I wouldn't have been able to do it, but now... I know you'll be completely professional. And frankly, I lost my modesty a long time ago. It's hard to be prudish when a photographer is adjusting your boobs in front of hundreds of people."

She saw that he still wasn't convinced. Well, neither was she. Not one hundred percent. "Here's the deal. I think once we get through the first exam, everything will be okay. But if it's not, I'll make other arrangements."

"Fair enough."

She looked at her jeans and T-shirt. "Do you want to do it now?"

"Nope. Not today. Today is blood tests and paperwork."

"Good."

He let go of her hands. "I'm going to send in Tracy, who does a terrific job of not hurting people. Then I'll come back to ask you some questions."

"Like *Jeopardy?*"

His chuckle made her tummy tighten. "If you like. But I think it will go faster if I just ask them the normal way."

"Spoilsport."

He turned to leave, but she wasn't ready for him to go yet. "Hey, Maitland."

"Yeah?"

"You still eat peanut butter every day?"

"Not *every* day. But I confess, there are times—"

"When you get out the tablespoon?"

"It's a perfectly harmless fetish."

"Bologna and peanut butter sandwiches are not harmless. They've been proven to blind laboratory rats."

"You forgot. Bologna, peanut butter and mayonnaise."

She shuddered dramatically. Then she caught his gaze again, and the temperature in the room shot up about ten degrees. "Do you have someone?" she asked, just as surprised as he was at the abrupt segue.

"Someone?"

She needed to know. Now. Whatever the answer was, it would be okay. In fact, it might be better all around if he was taken. "You know," she elaborated, keeping her tone light as a feather, "a wife."

He swallowed hard enough for her to notice his Adam's apple. "No. I did have, once."

"Oh." She waited for him to go on, but he didn't. She thought about prodding him, but it wouldn't be right. He was her doctor. She hoped he'd be her friend. Neither of which gave her any right to ask him about his private life.

Anxious to change the subject, she jumped from the table. "Do I have a minute before the vampire comes?"

"Of course."

"Good. I need to make a quick phone call."

"Use the phone here. Just dial nine to get out."

To get to the wall phone, she would have to pass him. Fully expecting him to leave, she went forward, but he stayed right where he was. So close that she had to turn sideways. So close that their bodies touched.

A memory came over her, so strong it was as if it had happened only yesterday. They'd won at the science fair. She'd wrapped her arms around his neck, and he'd touched her bare back. Her breasts, so new and so sensitive, had pressed against his chest. She'd felt the first flush of what it was like to be a woman that day. She'd felt it, and it had scared the hell out of her.

She'd jumped away from him, and sure enough, he hadn't been able to leave fast enough. She knew she'd embarrassed him, and the knowledge had kept her up nights. But along with the shame there was excitement, too. A secret thrill that had changed the way she felt about Mitchell Maitland forever.

Now the thrill was back. Back, and sixteen years stronger. The urge to wrap her arms around his neck was incredibly strong. They'd never kissed. Not really. Not a grown-up, set-your-hair-on-fire kiss.

His eyes darkened and then his mouth opened, and she felt sure that kiss was about to happen. She waited for his touch. Closed her eyes. Leaned forward until her breasts touched his chest.

He touched her back with his fingers. But only for a second. Even with her eyes closed she could sense his recoil. He almost tripped over a chair in his hurry to get away from her.

"I'll go get Tracy," he said, making it to the door in record time.

"Great," she said, as if nothing at all had happened.

After he closed the door behind him, she slumped against the table. Nothing at all *had* happened. Except for the realization that this wasn't going to be easy. The feelings she had for Mitch were more complicated than she'd imagined. She had a hell of a lot to think about.

CHAPTER FIVE

PETEY TURNED AWAY from *Wheel of Fortune,* pressed the mute button then tossed the remote on the couch. "I'll do it tonight," he said. "Wait till she's walking home. Then, bam, I'll get her before she knows what hit her."

"No, no, no." Janelle shook her head, impatient with his knee-jerk reaction. "We have to be careful. Think this through."

"But what if she wakes up? You know, loses her amnesia or whatever. She could nail you."

"Me? Not me alone, buddy boy."

"Yeah, yeah. That's what I meant."

Petey went to the kitchen and got another Corona out of the fridge. She watched him open it, then practically drain the bottle in one long drink. Her gaze went to his throat as he swallowed, and a little tickle started deep inside her.

He might not be an Einstein, but he was the sexiest thing she'd ever seen. He had the right equipment and he knew how to use it. If only he'd stop trying to think, everything would be perfect.

"I can do it, babe. I can. You don't know, but I'm real good with a knife."

"This isn't carving a turkey, Petey. It's killing

someone, and there can be no mistakes. Not one fingerprint, not one fiber.''

He came back to the living room and sat on the leather chair across from Janelle. Though it was small, the place was the nicest by far they'd ever stayed in. The art was ugly, but the rest of the guest house was just like something out of *House Beautiful*.

Janelle was going to take that silver ashtray when she left, and the crystal vase on the mantel, too. The Maitlands would never miss them. "Listen, here's what we have to do," she said as she brushed an errant strand of hair from her face. "You have to go by Austin Eats and check things out. Just make sure nobody sees you. Then you trail her when she leaves, try and figure out her schedule.''

Petey nodded, as if that had been his plan all along. She almost said something, then she figured it wouldn't do any good. As long as he kept on doing what she said, they'd be okay. And Lacy would disappear once and for all.

MITCH TURNED OFF his Dictaphone after the fourth mistake in five minutes. His mind wasn't on his charts. The situation with Darcy wouldn't let him be.

For a man who prided himself on his cool logic, he was working himself into a sweat. There was no way he would be Darcy's doctor if his feelings for her could in any way compromise the situation. This morning, when she'd touched him...

It was inappropriate, of course, but was it real? Was his desire for her a phantom from his past, or was he attracted to the Darcy of today?

Logic said his reactions were entirely based in the

past. How could it be otherwise? He didn't know
Darcy. Her life had changed her, just as his life had
changed him. They weren't kids anymore, so why
was he acting like one?

A knock on the door startled him. "Come in."

Abby poked her head in. "Are you busy?"

He looked at the stack of files he had to get
through. Then he sighed, knowing he was too distracted to work. "Come on in."

His sister sat across from him, and for the next ten
minutes they discussed a patient. He expected her to
leave in her usual abrupt manner—marriage hadn't
changed her that much. She still did more than any
two people he knew. But she put her file down and
settled in her chair.

"What's this?"

"I'm just curious."

"About?"

"Darcy."

He picked up the Dictaphone mike. "You know
why she's here."

"Yes, I do. But what I'm curious about is you."

"Me?"

"Is it uncomfortable?"

"Talking about her like this? Yes."

"No, is it uncomfortable, her being here? When
she left, you were pretty miserable."

"I was a teenager. What did you expect?"

She smiled and shook her head. "You know perfectly well it went beyond that. Remember that New
Year's Eve?"

He did. Unfortunately. He'd poured his heart out

to his younger sister, a result of too much champagne and not enough sense.

"As I recall, you said you still loved her. That was two years after she'd gone."

"Hormones. Nothing more."

"Not likely. You were smitten, big brother. And what I want to know is if you're still smitten?"

"Don't be ridiculous, Abby. Now, go on and get out of here. I've got work to do."

"Okay." She got up and went to the door, but she turned to face him. "Want to know what I think?"

"No."

"I think she's still smitten with you."

"What?"

"You heard me. I think she's come back to have a baby. But whether she knows it or not, artificial insemination isn't her first choice."

"You're insane."

"Ignore a woman's intuition at your peril. It's a strong and powerful force, Mitchell. Rarely wrong."

"It is this time."

She slipped out, but he heard her laugh before the door shut.

If he'd been confused before his sister's visit, he was twice that now. Was it possible Darcy had come back for him? No. Abby was still so swept up in her own love story that she wanted the rest of the world to be in love, too. It was a case of rose-colored glasses, that's all.

But damn it, he wished she hadn't planted that seed in his brain. It was going to be hell trying to forget it.

DARCY RAN her fingertips along the white wall in the nursery. Or what would be the nursery, if everything worked out. In her mind's eye she could see the bassinet, the Winnie-the-Pooh murals that would transform the white walls into a magical glade where Tigger and Roo and all her other favorite characters played.

There was nothing she wouldn't give her child. But none of the material things she could provide were half as important as a loving home and family.

She'd thought about waiting to see if she could find a man who would be part of that family, but it was a huge risk. She was too famous. There wasn't a thing she could do about it now. But, if she kept out of the limelight, her fame would fade until she was just an item in a book of trivia. Which was all she wanted.

Not that she was complaining. Her life had been extraordinarily privileged, and she knew it. Not only had she seen the world, but she'd learned a great deal about human nature on her travels. She saw how dangerous it was to have a lot of money and easy access to every sin. She also saw how beauty was a double-edged sword. It made life easy—everyone wanted to be around beautiful people, to do things for them. But it also made life scary, too. She was never sure the men she dated liked her, let alone loved her.

Maybe that was why she'd found herself thinking of Mitch so much these past six months. He'd always liked her, even when the other kids in school had called her String Bean and Flatty. The only fight he'd been in through school was over her. And he'd done darn well, too. She remembered how he'd worn his black eye with pride, even though Megan had grounded him for two weeks.

Oh, God. She was doing it again. It was nice to be back where she belonged, but the memories had to stop. How could she make any forward decisions when she was always looking backward? She couldn't let her happiness, or the happiness of her child, be dependent on the Maitland family or anyone else.

The doorbell interrupted her thoughts, and she headed downstairs, her footfalls echoing off the empty walls.

She opened the door for her agent, Hank, and saw the stretch limo in front of her house. She'd have to remind him to ride in something less obtrusive in the future.

"Could you be more in the suburbs?" he asked.

"Hello to you, too."

"I don't want to say hello." He walked past her into the house and looked around the foyer. Dressed to the nines in Armani silks, he looked at least ten years younger than his sixty years. "I'm still not speaking to you."

"Hank, honey, get over it. It's not as if I'm leaving you penniless."

He turned on her, and his dark blue eyes looked wounded. "You think that's what I'm worried about?"

"No, no and no. I'm sorry. It was supposed to be a flippant remark, but it just ended up stupid." She took his hands in hers and kissed his right cheek, then his left. "Forgive me?"

"Only for the remark," he said, his voice as petulant as his frown. "I don't forgive you for quitting."

"That's what I love about you. You beat a dead horse better than anyone I know."

"Smart-ass."

She grinned. "Ah, Hank. You always did know the right things to say."

He snorted, then headed toward the kitchen. She had to hurry to catch up to him. Even though he was four inches shorter than she was, he walked faster than anyone she'd ever met. Hank Fielding was the best agent in the business, as far as she was concerned. He'd taken care of her since she was seventeen, and was more of a father to her than her own had been. But Hank was also stubborn as a mule, and he believed it wasn't smart to quit in the middle of her contract with Avelon Cosmetics. He was worried about the repercussions, but since she didn't intend to model again, ever, what difference did it make? It wasn't as if Avelon would miss her. There were a hundred girls twice as beautiful waiting in line for the job.

He got to the kitchen and she saw his brow rise at her Sub-Zero fridge and her six-burner stove. "Claudia Schiffer has a palace in Majorca. Cindy Crawford has a penthouse in Manhattan, and a place in Telluride. You have to pick Austin, Texas?"

"What's the matter with Austin?"

"It's not New York, Paris or Majorca."

"You are a snob."

"Damn right I'm a snob. I've earned every snobbish thought wiping the noses of little girls like you."

"Hank, I'm not a little girl anymore. I'm thirty-four. Ancient for a model."

"Honey, with your looks, you could be on top for another ten years, easy."

She shook her head. "Sit down. Want a root beer?"

"When have I ever not wanted a root beer?"

She got two silver cans from the fridge and took them to the table, handing one to Hank and popping open the top of the other for herself.

He looked at the can, then at her. "What, were you raised by wolves? No glass, no ice?"

"My glasses aren't here yet. Pottery Barn is delivering tomorrow. So I don't think it would do too much good to give you ice."

He sighed, as if the deprivation bordered on torture.

And then he raised that damn right brow. "Still getting a Popsicle, eh?"

She laughed. "Frozen sperm from a donor, Hank. Which, if there's any mercy, will meet a nice egg and become my child."

"In my day, we did things the old-fashioned way. The girls got knocked up by the boys down the street."

A quick image of Mitchell came to mind, and her thoughts leapfrogged over logic to a place where he was the father of her baby.

"What's wrong?"

"Huh?"

"You got the funniest look on your face."

She shook the image from her head and focused on Hank. "Nothing. I'm fine."

He looked around the sparse kitchen. "You have a bed yet?"

"Not yet. But any minute. Tonight will be my first night here."

"Sure I can't convince you to come back to the hotel?"

She shook her head. "No. I'm dying to sleep here, even though I don't have glasses."

"Crazy." He leaned over and kissed her gently on the cheek. "But good as gold. If only..."

"Let's leave it at that, okay?"

"Can I ask one more thing?"

She nodded.

"What happens if this baby thing doesn't work out? Are you still going to want to live in Austin for the rest of your life?"

"It will work out. You wait and see. You'll be a godfather before you know it."

"I hope so, sweetheart. For your sake. Although when the news gets out that you've retired..."

"You won't let it out. Not yet. The last thing I need is the press hounding me here. God forbid they should find out about the baby. No, no. We're going to be very careful about that."

"Right. You know I'd never say a word."

"That I do. Now, want to see the rest of the house?"

MITCHELL SMILED at the reporter from the Austin *American-Statesman*, even though she was the last person in the world he wanted to talk to. It was late, he was hungry, and she wanted to know about the gala, which he'd done his level best to ignore.

He'd never have agreed to talk to her if his mother hadn't been out of town. Abby had ducked out, Beth had gone with Megan, and R.J.—well, R.J. had had his share of talking to the press these days. Mitch was beginning to wish he'd arranged to see her at his office, though, not his home.

"I understand there will be a few celebrities in attendance."

Mitch nodded. "Quite a few, yes."

The woman, Carolyn Jessup, waited, obviously expecting him to elaborate.

"Um, Clint Black and his wife. Madeline Stowe and Brian Benben. Let's see, Cybil Sheppard is supposed to be there, and I believe the Bush family will stop by."

"It sounds like the Oscars."

"We're hoping it's as exciting." He had to remember what his mother had told him, even though he'd only half paid attention. "We'll be having one of the finest chefs in Austin cooking for us. And all the flowers will be native to Texas."

"Sounds expensive."

"It's going to be very special. We owe a lot to the community, and we're honored to be able to celebrate our twenty-fifth-anniversary in grand Texas style."

She wrote on her pad, and his gaze went to his yearbook, which he'd left on the table last night. Sitting on top was the old picture of him with Darcy. He should have put it away. The last thing he wanted was for the reporter to—

"Is this who I think it is?" she asked, plucking the fading photograph from the table.

Mitch reached out to take it, but Carolyn Jessup pulled it out of reach.

"It is. It's Darcy Taylor. I remember now, she's from Austin." Her gaze went to him, and he saw a new and unsettling eagerness in her eyes. "Are you two...friends?"

The way she said it made him nervous. She wasn't asking if they were friends, she was asking if there was something newsworthy going on. "We were, many years ago."

"There are rumors going around about her, you know. That there's trouble with the Avelon contract."

"I wouldn't know about that."

"So you're not friends."

"She's a patient, and as such, I don't think I should—" He stopped talking as the horror of what he'd just said hit him. He'd broken Darcy's confidence, told the reporter, and therefore the whole world, that Darcy was a patient at Maitland Maternity.

Carolyn Jessup stood so quickly she knocked the photo to the carpet. Mitch got it first. By the time he looked up, she was halfway to the front door. "Wait, Ms. Jessup—"

"Thank you for your time," she said, not even bothering to face him in her hurry to get out. "I'm sure the gala will be wonderful."

"You can't print that about Darcy."

"Good night, Dr. Maitland."

"Please, I'm begging you!"

She stopped at his front door and gave him one last look that told him everything. Then she was gone, and he was in such deep trouble, he didn't know whether to laugh or leave the country.

He couldn't believe what he'd done. The one person in the world he would never want to hurt. Or betray. And he'd done both.

She'd never forgive him. She'd leave again, and that would be that. Any fantasies he'd had of continuing their friendship had vanished with a few simple words.

He was a fool. A damn stupid fool. There was only one thing he could think to do. He headed for the phone. His mother was the only person he knew who might be able to nip this in the bud. If he could reach her.

He had to try three different numbers before he could find her. By the time Megan answered, he wondered if his slip of the tongue had been more than that.

Was this his way of forcing Darcy to leave?

CHAPTER SIX

MITCH HUNG UP the phone, wondering if he'd gotten the number wrong. He'd dialed the number Darcy had given on her medical form, but there was no answer. There hadn't been an answer all morning, or last night. Perhaps she was staying at a hotel, but which one?

It was a little after noon, and he didn't have another patient until one-thirty. He should go to lunch, but he wasn't very hungry. Guilt. He'd had a terrible night's sleep, and already this morning he'd barked at a nurse and spilled hot coffee on his trousers. His curses had startled the lab tech, and she'd stared at him in shock.

He picked up the phone again, but this time he called his mother. She answered on the second ring. "Have you made any headway?"

Her pause gave him his answer. "Not yet," she said, confirming his suspicion. "I've talked to the managing editor," she went on, her voice calm even though he knew she must be terribly upset. "He won't budge. I put in a couple of other calls, but I wouldn't count on it. Have you spoken to Darcy?"

"She hasn't answered her phone."

"Keep trying, honey. She needs to be warned. If this hits the papers..."

"I'll find her," he said.

His mother paused again. Then she said, "I have great faith that things are going to be fine. Darcy is a remarkable woman. Although I know this is going to be uncomfortable for her, in the end it will work out. I just know it."

"And what if it doesn't?"

"You can't think like that, Mitchell. You take responsibility for your mistake, but you also have to recognize that it was a mistake. I know you. You're probably condemning yourself to hell and back."

He sighed. He had done exactly that.

"But stop it. Do your best to find her. Explain what happened. Together, the two of you can work out a solution."

"Okay. Thanks, Mother."

"Oh, and Mitchell?"

"Yes?"

"Go eat lunch. Even if it's just a quick bowl of soup."

He laughed. She knew him too well. "When will you be back?"

"Tonight."

"I'll speak to you then."

After she said goodbye, he tried calling Darcy's number again. It rang eighteen times before he gave up. If he was going to grab that lunch, he had to do it now. He'd take his cell phone and call her from Austin Eats.

DARCY WALKED toward the mall exit. Her deliveries were scheduled for this afternoon, and she needed to be home. She adjusted the bags in both hands, amazed that she'd managed to spend a small fortune in such a short time. But she was happy with what she had. Particularly the fireplace candles. She planned on having real fires in winter, but when it was warm out, she liked the idea of having eight tiered candles glowing behind the ornate screen she'd picked up in Montreal. They would look beautiful.

She glanced to her right and slowed as she saw she was in front of a baby shop. The stroller in the window was adorable! It was made to look like a bright yellow cartoon taxicab. As she stepped inside the store, she promised herself she'd only be a few minutes.

A saleswoman smiled at her, and Darcy nodded but didn't encourage her to come over. The last thing she wanted was to be spotted in this kind of shop. She transferred her bags to one hand and adjusted her hat and sunglasses. She felt foolish, but until things settled down she wanted no speculation.

Of course it would all come out eventually, but she wanted that done on her time, not the paparazzi's.

She headed toward the cradles in the back of the store, but she was sidetracked by a Winnie-the-Pooh revolving lamp. It would be perfect for the nursery, and she bent to pick it up. But she stopped short. There wasn't going to be a nursery until she got pregnant. Anything sooner, she felt, was tempting fate. The lamp would still be here. If not, she'd find something even better.

It was time to leave before she talked herself into doing something she shouldn't. There was so much that had to go right, and the least little thing might spoil it. Hank would say it was all superstitious nonsense, but Hank never wanted to be a mother.

MITCH SAT in his usual seat at the counter, the one farthest from the kitchen, where he could read in peace. Although today he hadn't brought a book or a journal. He couldn't have paid attention if he tried.

"How are you?"

He looked up to see Shelby Lord, the owner of Austin Eats, smiling at him.

"I'm fine," he said, lying through his teeth. "How about you?"

She shrugged. "Fine, too, if you mean sort of miserable by fine."

He smiled. "Yeah. That's just what I mean. What's your beef?"

"Nothing a winning lottery ticket wouldn't fix."

"Ah," he said. "Do you need some help? I could—"

She held up her hand. "No, but thank you. I'll work it out. I always do."

"I thought business was going well."

"It is. It's my house that's not. I need a new roof and I need a new hot water heater."

"Ouch."

"Who got hurt?" Sara asked, approaching.

"My pocketbook," Shelby replied, smiling at her new chef. They were such a contrast. Shelby with her startling red hair and expressive eyes stood a good three inches taller than Sara, with her shoulder-length blond hair and blue eyes. Both were attractive in their own way, but he had the feeling Shelby wasn't terribly comfortable with her looks. He wasn't sure why he thought that, but he did.

"What'll you have, Doc?" Sara asked.

"I thought you were the new chef?"

"I am. But not today. Mary Jane is out sick."

"I'll just have my usual."

"You got it." Sara wrote on her little pad as she walked to the kitchen window.

"I heard a rumor," Shelby said, setting him up with silverware and water.

"What?".

"That Darcy Taylor is in town. In fact, that she's been to the clinic."

He felt his throat go dry. It couldn't have hit the papers yet, could it? "Where did you hear that?"

Shelby took a quick step backward. "Whoa. What's wrong?"

"Nothing," he said, trying to keep his cool. "Just...please. Where did you hear that?"

"I was teasing. Abby and Darcy were here the other day for lunch."

He exhaled and felt his blood pressure go down. "Listen, Shelby, if anyone comes around..."

"You think I would say anything? I value all my customers too much to do something as stupid as that."

Sara started back from the service window with his lunch—a peanut butter and jelly sandwich on white bread with a small salad. "What's stupid?"

Shelby shook her head. "Nothing."

Sara put down his plate. "There you go, Connor."

"Who?" he asked.

"What?" she responded, clearly unaware of what she'd done.

Shelby put a glass of milk by his plate, then turned to Sara. "You called him Connor."

"I did?"

Mitchell nodded. "Do you know my mother's nephew?"

"Not really." Sara's brows came down. "I actually called you Connor?"

Given that he'd just taken a bite of his sandwich, he could only nod again.

"That's odd."

"Do you think it was just a slip or a memory?" Shelby asked. "Someone from your past, maybe?"

"Who knows?" Sara sounded despondent.

Mitch swallowed and sipped some milk, then said, "Maybe it was Connor O'Hara you were thinking about. Maybe you overheard someone say his name recently."

"He's your cousin, right? The baby's father."

"Yeah. He just showed up last fall out of the blue." Mitch swallowed another bite, surprised at his hunger. "Next time I see him, I'll ask him to stop by. You never know. He might have some answers for you."

Sara sighed. "Wouldn't that be nice?"

"Mitchell," Shelby said. "You're buzzing."

He looked at his beeper. It was his secretary. Maybe she'd heard from Darcy.

PETEY DUCKED behind the building as Mitchell Maitland stepped out of the diner. After waiting a couple of minutes, Petey checked to make sure the coast was clear. It was.

He pulled his baseball cap down lower on his forehead, stuck his hands in his bomber jacket and walked slowly past the window.

The place was packed, and it took him a while to

find Lacy. Damn, she was so pretty—he'd like to get some of that himself. Maybe…

She looked his way, and he moved on, not hurrying at all. Just sort of strolling.

Janelle didn't want him to off her yet. He hadn't argued. Sometimes Janelle could be real smart about stuff. But he was smart, too.

He was the one who had to do the messy work, not her. She'd screwed up, and now it was his turn. He wouldn't screw up. In fact…

He looked at Lacy again. She was laughing about something. Damn, but she was fine. Maybe he'd have a little fun with her before he finished her off. Why not? It was all his ball game here, not Janelle's.

Janelle thought he was a fool. Oh, she tried to hide it, but he could see it in her eyes. She thought he was a dummy just because he didn't finish school. That wasn't his fault, though. His old man had died, and where did that leave him? In charge of feeding a family of four. His mother hadn't done squat except sit at home and drink. The other kids, all younger than him, had depended on Petey for the food on the table, for the roof over their heads. A dummy couldn't have done that. Not at sixteen. He'd worked so damn hard. Every morning, before the sun came up, he was at the dockyard, doing the kind of work no man wanted to do. Cleaning fish guts, moving barrels. It had toughened him up, though. And when he'd left the docks for construction work, he'd taken those skills and used them well.

Now it was his turn. He was going to play a little cat-and-mouse game with Lacy, and then he'd do her.

And he'd do her right. That would show Janelle who she was dealing with.

After he'd finished with Lacy, he'd have to decide once and for all. Was he going to stay with Janelle, or was he going to fix it so that she disappeared, too? Of course, being married, all the money would come to him.

It wasn't that he didn't like Janelle, because he did. He just got tired sometimes of her bossing him around.

It wasn't going to be easy to decide. So he'd think about it for a while. In the meantime, he was going to have himself a good old time.

Lacy wouldn't know what hit her.

DARCY TURNED onto her new street, her mind occupied with dishes and candles and linens and babies. But as she approached her house, all those thoughts vaporized. The *Tattle Today TV* news van was the first thing that made her stomach tense. Then she saw the crowd of reporters, the cameras, the microphones. A delivery truck was in the driveway, and there was a throng of bottom feeders surrounding the driver.

Her heart thudded in her chest as she turned her Bronco sharply to the left, into a driveway, then backed out to make her escape. How had they found out? What the hell had happened?

It had to be someone from Maitland. No one else except Hank knew about her being there, and or where her house was. Some nurse or maybe that receptionist had probably called the *Tattle Today TV* woman. From what Abby and Beth had told her,

Maitland had been under a lot of scrutiny ever since the baby had been discovered on the clinic steps.

Darcy turned onto Willow Street, threw her sunglasses on the passenger seat and wiped her eyes with the back of her hand. She should have known better! She'd heard all about the scandal that had rocked Maitland. Of course there would be reporters! What was she thinking?

She took another turn, not noticing the street name, no destination in mind. Her lovely day, her lovely home, her lovely dreams were all gone. Taken from her by selfishness and greed.

Tears blurred her vision, so she pulled into a gas station and parked the car. The wide-brimmed white hat she'd used as a disguise was useless, and she tossed it into the back seat.

Mourning the loss of her privacy, she watched as cars drove in and cars drove out.

After a while, the self-pity eased, and in its place came anger. Pure, bright, burning anger.

It had never ceased to amaze her that she was a celebrity. All she'd given the world was good bone structure and a mannequin's body. That's all. She'd never really done anything worth anything. And yet, they wanted so much of her.

She'd been hounded by the press for so long, she hardly remembered a life before it. She never should have taken the cover of *Sports Illustrated.* Or the Victoria's Secret campaign. And she never should have dated George Clooney.

But damn it, they had no *right.* This was her life. She owed them nothing! Not interviews, not pictures, and most of all not her privacy.

She put the Bronco in gear and headed east. Mitchell would help her. He'd be just as upset as she was that someone from Maitland had leaked confidential information. She wouldn't be half surprised if someone got fired as a result of this. It was inexcusable. And it was just plain depressing.

MITCH FOUND HER in his office. She stood by the window, staring at the big oak. Dressed in unadorned jeans and a plain T-shirt, her hair pulled back in a ponytail, she looked impossibly young and vulnerable. When she turned and he saw the red around her eyes, he felt like pond scum. He'd done this to her. He'd hurt her deeply, and she had every reason in the world not only to never speak to him again, but to sue the pants off Maitland.

"I know you're busy," she said as she walked toward him. "But I need your help."

"Darcy—"

"Someone told the press I was here," she said, as if she hadn't heard him. "It must have been someone from here, because no one else knew."

Before he could stop her, she'd rested her head on his shoulder and put her hands around his waist. He groaned, cursing his stupidity, appalled that at a moment like this his body stirred at her nearness.

He took hold of her arms and gently pushed her back. "Darcy."

She sniffed.

"Darcy... Oh, God. I'm so sorry."

"It's not your fault."

"Yes. Yes, it is my fault."

"Mitchell, you can't help it if someone picked up the phone—"

"Darcy," he said, much more sharply than he meant to.

She jerked back, her eyes wide with surprise.

"Listen to me," he said, raising his voice. "*I'm* the one that leaked the information."

The surprise in her gaze changed to confusion, and then to the deepest sadness he'd ever seen in his life. She stepped away from him and turned her back.

He'd blown it big time.

CHAPTER SEVEN

SHE COULDN'T believe it. Not Mitch. But when she turned to face him, she saw that it was true. He'd done it. He felt badly about it, but that didn't change anything.

"I can't tell you how sorry I am," he said. "I'd give anything to take it back. It was stupid. The reporter found your picture and she insinuated that we...that I..." He shook his head, and Darcy noticed his hair wasn't combed. It looked as if he'd run his fingers through it many times, and it stuck up in back.

Her thoughts jerked back to the fix she was in. How was she going to get through this if the whole world was watching? Trying to conceive would be hard enough without progress reports in every paper across the country.

"We tried to stop them from printing the story, but they wouldn't hear of it."

She leaned back so she was half-sitting on his desk. "They're all over my house like a swarm of bees. When I drove by, they'd surrounded the Pottery Barn deliveryman. He's probably still stuck there."

"Can't the police—"

"No. The police can't do anything. I'm a public figure, and that means I'm fair game. I can't do a damn thing about it."

"Maybe if you explained…"

She shook her head, the thought of facing the press with her most personal business making her sick to her stomach. "I'll check back into a hotel. Eventually, they'll leave me alone."

"No. That's not going to work. You'd be recognized instantly."

"So what do you suggest I do? Find a convenient cave to hide in?"

His eyes changed while she watched him. Just like in the old days. Mitch could never hide the fact that he'd had an inspired idea, whether it was the answer to a trigonometry problem or a way to sneak out of church. For the first time since she'd turned onto her street, she felt a little hopeful.

"You're not going to stay in a cave. But it'll be close. You'll stay with me."

"Pardon?"

"You'll stay at my house. It's a gated community. No one who doesn't belong is going to get in."

"You underestimate the paparazzi. They can get in anywhere."

"We'll make sure they don't."

"I don't know." She stood, unable to keep still. "Maybe I should just tell everything. They'll write about it for a little while, then it'll blow over."

Mitch went around his desk and sat down. She could see from his expression that he had decided the course of action and that he'd be very hard to dissuade. But she wasn't sure. "If you want to tell them, that's one thing," he said. "But you don't have to. It's your business, Darcy. No one else's. You have the right to do this privately."

"It doesn't matter if I have the right. They're like pit bulls, those reporters. They get hold of a story and they don't let go."

"The gala is coming up in less than two weeks. We're having celebrities from here to tomorrow flying in. The press is going to have a field day. They'll be too busy to worry about you."

"Swell, but that still means we have at least a week to get through."

"We'll think of something. The important thing is not to worry. I've got a guest bedroom. We'll get your things from your house, and I guarantee no one will be the wiser."

"I don't know—"

He sprang up, walked right to her and put his hands on her arms. His touch made her gasp, not with pain but with the surge of electrical energy flowing from him to her. "I got you into this. I'll get you out. Even if I have to personally shred every damn journalist in Texas."

All she could do was nod. This was a Mitchell she didn't know. The man he'd become while she was away. Totally confident. Completely self-contained. And utterly masculine.

"Darcy—" His grip tightened, sending heat through her body. She knew he was going to pull her close and kiss her. She could see it in his eyes, feel it in his hands.

But he let her go. He stepped away so fast he knocked into the guest chair. His gaze was the last thing to disconnect, and she understood what she saw there, too. Because she felt the same thing.

She shouldn't stay with him. It was too dangerous.

She was vulnerable around Mitch, and it was too easy to let nostalgia cloud her thinking.

But what if it wasn't wishful thinking? What if they were meant to be together? What if destiny was moving the pieces of their lives?

She needed to know—one way or the other—before she went on with the insemination. She had to know if these feelings coursing through her were real. And if the smoldering heat in his gaze would become a steady flame.

PETEY HUNG UP the phone and glowered at Janelle. "That was Mitchell Maitland."

"What'd he want?"

"He told me that his friend Sara said the name Connor in the middle of serving him his lunch."

Janelle, who had enough whiskey in her to sink a battleship, sat bolt upright in bed. "Tell me everything. Don't leave anything out."

"Now, why you gotta say something like that? I don't ever leave anything out, and you know it."

"Fine. You don't leave anything out," she said, her words slurred but her eyes as focused as a laser beam. "So tell me."

"He said she was serving him some food, and she called him Connor."

"Oh, shit," Janelle said, reaching for her glass. "We gotta move faster than I thought."

"I told you I'm taking care of her."

"Yeah? What's your plan?"

"I'm not finished with it yet."

"If you tell me what you've got so far, I can help."

"I know your kind of help. You'll change everything. You'll call my ideas stupid."

"Oh, for God's sake, Petey, this isn't a competition. We could fry for this. So what's better, you feeling like you're a big man, or we get out of this with our money and our lives?"

He didn't answer her. It wouldn't have done any good. But the way she was acting lately? He might have to shut her up. Get her out of his hair.

On the other hand, maybe she'd straighten up as soon as he showed her what he could really do. Which meant he'd better get a move on.

He went to the bedroom mirror and combed his hair. "I do look like one of them Maitlands," he said. "Only better-looking."

"You got that right, sugar," Janelle agreed. "So how about you go get us another bottle?"

"Haven't you had enough?"

"I'll tell you when I've had enough."

"All right, all right. Jeez."

"And when you get back, we'll talk about the next step, right? We'll talk it through."

"Yeah," he said. "Sure." And then he turned to go into the kitchen, cursing under his breath. He'd show her. He would show her big time.

DARCY LOCKED the dead bolt, then looked out the peephole one last time before she let herself relax. She turned to get her first look at Mitchell's town house.

She liked it immediately. It was sleek and elegant, but inviting, too.

The foyer had black and white tiles, just like the

tiles at the Maitland mansion. Was it coincidence? Fresh flowers had been arranged beautifully on an antique table, and she wondered if he had them delivered that way, or if that had been done by more familiar hands.

She walked to the living room, and her eye went straight to the painting above the couch. It wasn't a work she'd seen before, but she wished she had. Huge, abstract, gorgeous, the painting had tremendous energy. The room must have been decorated to go with the painting, not the other way around. The deep burgundy at the center was echoed in the thick carpet, in the curtains. But it wasn't dark or gloomy. There was too much vibrancy in the pillows on the couch and the glass sculptures on the end table and the credenza.

His chairs were big. Leather club chairs with ottomans, facing the fireplace. It would be lovely to read there, perhaps with a cup of tea and a nice cozy blanket over her lap.

It was a good space, and she was glad for Mitchell. Especially when she saw the pictures on the mantelpiece. His family were all there, Megan looking regal.

As her fingers touched the frame of the largest portrait, her chest ached with the pain she'd known forever. The feeling of distance, of being incredibly alone. She'd gone through life standing outside the window, staring with longing at the happy family that had been her ideal. She'd have her own family. She'd have children, and their portraits would be on the mantelpiece in her home. She'd make her own tribe, even though she had to start from scratch.

She headed toward the kitchen, but her gaze caught

the corner of a Polaroid picture on the end table next to the club chair. As she got closer, she realized it was a picture of her. Her and Mitchell. The day they'd won at the science fair.

Picking it up, she was startled at how young they both looked. How innocent. Mitchell was handsome back then. He still had a growth spurt to look forward to, and his face would change with maturity, but his eyes were the same. His expression. His intelligence.

He'd kept the picture all these years. This was the picture he'd referred to. The one the reporter had seen. Why had he left it out? She sighed at her own silliness. It meant nothing, for heaven's sake. She had come back after being away forever, and that had spurred him to take a trip down memory lane. Big deal.

She put the picture back and went to the kitchen. After she put the kettle on to boil, she looked around the roomy space. It was a good kitchen, with a gas stove, a work island and a cozy table in the corner. She laughed out loud when she saw the framed picture above the table. Albert Einstein, Mitch's hero. Only he would have a picture like that in the kitchen.

As she was about to sit, the doorbell rang, scaring her half to death. The press. They'd found her already. It wasn't fair. Wasn't there anywhere left to hide?

The doorbell rang again. She didn't have to open the door, right? But then she remembered that she'd taken Mitch's key. It was probably him.

The doorbell rang once more as she hurried to answer it. She looked out the peephole, only it wasn't

Mitch she saw. It wasn't the press, either. It was a little boy.

Cautiously, she opened the door. The boy, who seemed about nine or ten, gave her a puzzled look. "May I help you?" she asked.

"Is Dr. Mitch home?"

"No, I'm afraid he's not."

The boy's shoulders slumped in disappointment. What was this about?

"He was supposed to help me with my homework. He promised."

"What kind of homework?"

"Math."

She debated. "What's your name?"

"Adam. I live over there." He pointed to the town house next door.

"Well, Adam, I'm not Dr. Mitch, but I bet I could help you with your math homework."

He looked dubious. Very dubious.

"What's wrong?"

"You're a—"

"Girl?"

He nodded.

"Don't be so prejudiced. I may be a girl, but I know mathematics. I used to get better grades than Dr. Mitch."

"You did not."

She crossed her heart with her index finger. "Swear I did."

He didn't look convinced.

"Tell you what. Let's give it a try, and if I suck, you can always let Dr. Mitch help you later."

She watched him debate. His gaze went from her

to his house, then back. He shifted his backpack from one hand to the other. Finally, he nodded. "Okay."

"Come on in."

He did. She followed him to the kitchen, where he dumped his pack. Then he turned to face her. "Who are you?"

"My name is Darcy."

"Are you his girlfriend?"

"No. Just his friend. We went to school together."

"Oh."

"Can I get you something to drink before we start?"

"I'll do it." He went straight to a glass canister on the counter and got out three white-chocolate-chip cookies. Then he stood on tiptoe and got a glass. By the time he'd poured himself milk, picked up a napkin and settled at the table, her water boiled.

"You come here a lot?" she asked, knowing the answer had to be yes.

"Yeah."

"Just for homework?"

"I guess. But sometimes for other things."

"Like what?"

He shrugged. She understood. She didn't like prying questions, either. She brought her tea to the table, then she and Adam got to work.

An hour later, all his problems done and his understanding of fractions a bit more solid, Adam looked at her in a whole new way.

"See, I told you girls could do math."

He nodded. "Can you do science, too?"

She smiled. "I kick butt in science."

The boy smiled, and his cheeks grew very pink.

She had the feeling he just might be falling for her. But that was okay. She was falling for him, too.

"I gotta go," he said, stuffing his papers into his pack. "My mom'll kill me if I'm late for dinner."

"It was fun, Adam. I'm glad you came over."

"Darcy?"

"Yes?"

He stared hard at the salt shaker. "Could I come again?"

She nodded. "Dr. Mitch will be back later."

"No. I meant, to see...you?"

"Of course. But I have to warn you. I probably won't be staying long. A few days, I think."

"But you'll be here tomorrow?"

She nodded.

"Awesome." He shifted his backpack and headed toward the front door.

She liked him. He was a cutie, and he was bright. With his dark hair and his green eyes, he reminded her of Mitch at that age. So full of energy. So ready to take on the world.

He left, waving at her as he crossed the yard. She shut the door behind him, locked it, then her gaze went to the mantelpiece. To the family she would have someday. To her own son, her own daughter. And maybe, jut maybe, her own husband.

SHE WAS IN HIS PAJAMAS.

Sound asleep on the couch, Darcy was achingly beautiful. She'd covered herself with an afghan, but her feet stuck out at the bottom. Her hair swept over the pillow, and her cheek looked as smooth as satin.

He covered her toes, then picked up a paper bag

and one of her suitcases and headed for the guest room. The bed was still made, the curtains drawn. He wondered if she'd even been in here.

It wasn't a very feminine room. Funny he'd never noticed that before. The comforter was tartan, the walls hunter green. Maybe fresh flowers would make her more comfortable. He'd have another bouquet added to his usual delivery.

For now, though, he wanted to get her into bed. It was only eleven-fifteen, but she was clearly exhausted. So was he. Going to her house had been a job for James Bond, not him. He'd had to wait out most of the press, and then he'd had his secretary cause a diversion while he sneaked in the back.

That wasn't half as distressing, however, as opening her underwear drawer.

It was filled with white lace, black silk, red satin. He'd found it remarkably difficult not to imagine her in every one of the tiny garments. Of course, she hadn't made things any easier by being the centerpiece of that Victoria's Secret ad campaign a few years back. So even if he hadn't had any imagination at all, he could still picture her in far too much detail.

He'd ended up bringing everything. All the underwear in the drawer. All her makeup and hair stuff, too. As for clothes, he'd packed as much as he could, but the woman had more clothes than Neiman Marcus. He would have needed a truck to bring it all. And he'd taken one more thing. The time capsule. They'd open it tomorrow. Together.

He pulled down the corner of the comforter and headed to the living room to get the rest of her things. Just as he got hold of suitcase number two, she jerked

up, a half scream scaring him so thoroughly he
dropped her suitcase, which burst open, showering the
carpet and the coffee table with underpants and bras.

"Oh, God, you scared me."

"*I* scared *you?*"

She sat up on the couch, holding the afghan against
her chest. "I didn't mean to fall asleep. What time is
it?"

"Past eleven."

She rubbed the sleep from her eyes, then froze as
she saw her undergarments all over the floor. "I see
you got in my drawers," she said, a smile teasing her
lips at the intentional pun.

"And your closet," he replied, too unhinged to
tease back. He gathered the clothes and stuffed them
into the suitcase.

"Were the reporters there?"

He nodded. "No one saw me go in, though."

"They didn't see the lights?"

"I used a flashlight."

"Really?"

"Yeah. I'd make a pretty good cat burglar, I
think."

"Pity cats don't have anything good to burgle."

He stood up. "You're in rare form tonight."

"And I'm still half asleep. Hey, have you had dinner?"

"No. I've been too busy playing I Spy."

She tossed the afghan aside and got up. "I cooked.
I can heat it up in two seconds."

"Aren't you tired?"

"Not with all this adrenaline pumping through me.
Come on." She waved at him. "It's spaghetti," she

said, once they were in the kitchen. "You didn't have any vegetables, so I couldn't make any."

"Spaghetti sounds great."

"How about you pouring us each a glass of wine while I heat this up. Then I want to hear about life on the outside."

Mitch got a bottle of Merlot from his wine rack and watched her as he opened it. She moved around his kitchen as if she belonged there. Totally unself-conscious about her attire or the fact that her hair was all over the place. Or that she was the most exquisite woman he'd ever seen.

He didn't need the wine. Looking at her was enough to make him feel light-headed. His gaze moved down her long, lean body. Barefoot. As im-probable as it was, Darcy Taylor was cooking him dinner. In his pajamas. And her toenails were painted candy-apple red. *Damn.*

CHAPTER EIGHT

DARCY FINISHED heating the pasta and brought it to the table. There was a glass of wine on the place mat next to him, and that's where she sat.

"Thank you," he said, as if he couldn't believe she could boil water, let alone cook a meal.

"My pleasure."

He cleared his throat twice. "From what I saw, and believe me, it was a limited view, the old place looks great." He swirled spaghetti on his fork as he spoke.

"It is. The Kendricks took good care of it, and I had the whole place painted and the floors redone. Most of the furniture was supposed to be delivered today. I called and canceled almost everything. The truck just took my stuff back to the warehouse."

"I'm truly sorry, Darcy. I've made a real mess of things."

"Don't worry about it. Guilt is pretty worthless. What I need to do now is make a new plan, that's all."

"That's all?"

"Eat your dinner. Yes, that's all. Boulders fall in the road of life every day. So we have to go over them or around them or under them. The only time the boulder wins is if we give up."

A slow smile changed his face, making him even more appealing. "That's one heck of a philosophy."

She sipped some wine. He ate some spaghetti. The silence between them was cozy and comfortable, as if they hadn't been apart for a day, let alone sixteen years. "I wasn't born knowing that," she said finally. "In fact, all I ever saw from my parents were insurmountable problems."

"What changed?"

"It was a single decision on a single day." She set her wine down but kept her hands busy rubbing the crystal. "A single, awful, incredible day. I was in California, at the beach. I had been up for a major cosmetics contract, and I'd lost out to Cindy Crawford. My mother was in Las Vegas, ostensibly to find my father. She didn't, of course. But she did manage to go through almost a hundred thousand dollars."

His fork stopped halfway to his mouth. "Pardon?"

She nodded. "You'd think, after what we went through with my father, the last thing in the world she'd do was gamble."

"I didn't know that."

"What?"

"That your father had a gambling problem."

"Oh, yeah. But that's another story."

"Sorry. You were at the beach."

"Right. I was sitting on an almost deserted stretch of beach at Playa Del Rey. It was cold and windy. I stared at the ocean for a long time while I contemplated my future. One option was to quit. I mean, bigtime quit. End it all."

"Not really?"

"Yes, really. The other options were less permanent. Quit modeling. Move to Europe and go to school. Join the circus. It didn't matter, as long as I got away. And then it occurred to me that I would never get away. Wherever I went, I'd be there.''

''Wow.''

''Don't laugh. It was profound. It was a lightning bolt and it changed everything.''

''I wasn't laughing.''

She could see it was true. His eyes were filled with interest and concern, but he wasn't mocking her. ''Anyway, when that occurred to me, I knew that I had to make a decision. Since I'd be there for the rest of my life, I could approach that life either as a victim or as a winner. I chose the latter.''

''How old were you?''

''About twenty-one.''

His brows went up in surprise. ''That's young for such a wise decision.''

''Self-preservation, not wisdom. I'd read this quote from Abraham Lincoln. He said that people are about as happy as they make up their minds to be. I think that's the big truth.''

''So you kept on modeling, obviously.''

''Yep. But I also educated myself. I studied finance, and it turned out that I had a gift for it.''

''What kind of gift?''

She smiled, not without a certain amount of pride. ''I'm loaded.''

''Loaded?''

''Filthy, stinking rich.''

''No kidding?''

She sipped some more wine, savoring the warmth more than the rich taste. ''It's true. But not many people know. I'll never have to work again if I don't want to.''

"So you can devote your time to being a mother?'' She nodded.

"That's great, Darcy. I'm really happy for you.''

She put her hand over his. ''That's why you can't worry about this. Nothing is broken except Plan A. All that's necessary is to come up with Plan B.''

He laughed, shaking his head at a private joke.

"What?''

"It just hit me. You've grown up.''

"I should hope so.''

"No, I mean it. You're not the girl I knew before. You've become a woman. A very...beautiful woman.''

Heat came to her cheeks and she looked away, sud denly self-conscious about his pajamas and the fact that she had nothing on underneath them. It was lu dicrous—she knew what he meant, and it had nothing to do with sex. But obviously her body had a different interpretation, because her nipples tightened as if the temperature had dropped twenty degrees. ''So what about your day?'' she asked, desperate to shift the conversation to a safer topic.

"Except for worrying about you, not much. Wait. There was one thing that was kind of interesting.''

"Hmm?''

"I don't know if you met Sara at the diner?''

"I did. But very briefly.''

"I had lunch there today, just like always.''

"Peanut butter and jelly, right?''

"It's a perfectly legitimate lunch. Anyway, Sara

has been my waitress dozens of times. But today, she called me Connor.''

"And?''

He got up and put his empty plate in the sink. "You know she doesn't remember who she is, right?''

"Oh, so you think her calling you Connor is her memory coming back?''

"I'm not sure. But I think it's too much of a co-incidence to believe that Connor O'Hara showed up in Austin out of the blue, and then Sara calls me Connor. It's an unusual name.''

"Maybe he'd been there before. The diner, I mean.''

"Still, it's an odd slip. I called Connor and told him to make a point of stopping by Austin Eats. If her memory is returning…''

"Wouldn't that be something? Poor thing. I can't imagine how it must feel to forget your past. It would be sort of like being adrift at sea. No anchors.''

"It's possible that she'll regain her memory entirely. We know so little about amnesia. Sometimes, actually most times, amnesia isn't this kind. It can make a person forget more than memories. Things like speech or reading.''

She shuddered at the thought, then got up to put her glass in the sink. "I spoke to Beth today, by the way. She was telling me about the preparations for the gala. It sounds incredible.''

"It'll be a nightmare.''

"You think so?'' she said, but what she really wanted was for him to ask her to go with him.

"The press will be wall-to-wall. I don't want to

talk about the gala. That's what got us into this mess.''

''I told you, don't—''

''Worry. Yes, I know. But I'm constitutionally incapable of not worrying about certain things. This is one of them.''

She turned to him, folding her arms across her chest. ''Well, get over it.''

He laughed. ''Boy, some things haven't changed.''

''Like what?''

''Nothing.''

''Mitch!''

He headed for the living room. No way was she going to let him get away with that comment. She dashed after him and caught his arm just as he crossed the threshold.

Abruptly he turned around, his gaze going to her hand for a few seconds, as if he couldn't believe she was touching him. Then he looked at her, and she knew instantly that he was experiencing the sort of weirdness she had a few minutes ago. His eyes dilated, his breathing became rough and fast, and his mouth opened as if ready for a kiss.

She knew it was her touch that had sparked him, yet she didn't take back her hand. Instead, she stepped closer to him. Closer than was wise.

He brought his hand up, hesitated, then touched her cheek. A feathery light touch that sent a thrill of excitement all the way down to her toes. ''Oh, God.''

She nodded, sure she knew what he was thinking. Was this real? Was it possible? Was this just a continuation of a childhood crush, or something much deeper?

Sneaking his fingers behind her neck, he pulled her toward him. She felt his reaction through their clothes. She wasn't the only one who'd grown up. Mitchell was a man now, not an awkward teenager. His hand on her back was broad and strong, his chest solid. And he felt hard against the juncture of her thighs. Hard and hot, as hot as her own center. She moved her hips, and he groaned.

He leaned closer, a fraction of an inch away from a kiss. A kiss that never came. Mitch threw his head back in a gesture of pure frustration. In that moment, reality hit her squarely on the chin. This wasn't a good idea. Not now. Not when there were so many unanswered questions.

As if he'd felt her shift, he looked at her. She sighed. He nodded twice, then helped her stand again. Once she was on solid ground, he stepped away.

She wasn't sure if this was the right thing. Her body objected vigorously, but somewhere inside her a voice told her to wait. If something was to come of this, they needed time. Time and a level head, something she didn't have right now.

"There are towels in the guest bath," he said. "If you need anything else, let me know."

"Mitch?"

He didn't wait to hear more. He didn't turn to face her. He headed for the stairs and his bedroom.

Mitch was careful not to slam the door. He didn't want her to know how frustrated he felt, or that he was cursing himself for a fool yet again. He'd almost kissed her, for God's sake.

Why had he stopped?

If he'd pressed a little harder, she would have acquiesced. He was sure of it. He could have wiped her doubts away with a touch. But after what he'd done...

One thing for sure—being noble stunk. His whole body screamed for a release he couldn't have. Nothing would do but to be inside her, and that wasn't going to happen.

"Damn it," he said as he tore at his necktie. He finally got the stupid noose off and threw it on his dresser, then headed for the bathroom. He turned on the water in the sink and adjusted the temperature. He made it cold, even though he wasn't scientifically convinced that cold water would help in a situation like this. At least not cold water splashed on his face. If worse came to worst, he'd apply it elsewhere.

He shivered at the thought, then washed in the frigid water. Once that was done, he concentrated on brushing his teeth, but neither activity made him any more comfortable.

It was just like high school.

Darcy had made him hard at the drop of a hat. He'd had to carry his books with him at all times, just so he wouldn't humiliate himself in front of the whole school. She'd touch him, not meaningfully or anything, maybe just on the shoulder or on the back, and he'd spring to attention. It was a hell he'd thought he'd outgrown. A hell for pubescent boys with no self-control.

But he wasn't fifteen anymore. His hormones had learned to behave themselves. Well, to a large extent. But with Darcy, all bets were off. He wondered if he should start carrying a medical text around.

He spit out the toothpaste, then looked at himself in the mirror. His hair was a mess, his five-o'-clock shadow was going on midnight, and his eyes were tinged medical-resident red because he hadn't slept last night.

Very seductive. A real Casanova.

He cursed at his image. The day before yesterday, his life had been great. Nothing he couldn't handle. No one wearing his pajamas or bugging him about his peanut butter and jelly sandwiches.

The trouble in the family had finally worked itself out. Well, to a degree. He still wasn't sure about everyone's sanity. Abby had found Kyle, Ellie had found Sloan. Even R.J. was with his Dana now. The disease had spread outside the family, too. His friends Hope and Drake were together again, and Ford had finally snagged Katie Topper before it was too late. Even Beth had managed to find herself a fiancé, despite a murder investigation. And his sister Anna had her son, Will.

That left his brother Jake and him as the last bachelors. And for all he knew, Jake might be married with six kids. Which would leave Mitch as the lone standard-bearer for the single life.

He wasn't about to jump on the bandwagon, Darcy or no Darcy. After Angela's death, he'd made a decision very much like Darcy's that day on the beach. He wasn't going to marry again. He'd been a terrible disappointment to Angela, whether she'd admitted it or not. He'd seen the look in her eyes. She'd known about the problems with the pregnancy. She'd asked him to make things better, but he'd failed. He'd made a vow to himself that night. Never again...

Just because he wanted Darcy was no reason to forget the lessons life had taught him.

So why did he still want Darcy?

Of course he wanted her. Who didn't? She was the object of millions of fantasies. Her pictures graced thousands of walls, and countless young girls had done everything in their power to look like her.

If he *hadn't* wanted her, he'd have been worried.

Back in his bedroom, he finished changing into his pajamas. Before he climbed between the sheets, he opened the door, just a crack. It was dark. He ventured to the stairwell. Everything was still. As quietly as he could, he went down the stairs, avoiding the fourth step, which creaked.

At the landing, he could see the guest room. No light came from between the cracks. She was in bed. Probably sleeping soundly. Probably dreaming of Richard Gere or Brad Pitt or someone like that.

Not him.

Darcy had come home for a reason. She wanted to have a child, and she wanted to have it alone. Her reaction to him was purely nostalgic and had nothing to do with the man he was now or the woman she'd grown to be.

Which was a shame. Because he liked her. Because he wanted to get to know her. But that wouldn't be a very bright thing to do. Because he knew without a shadow of a doubt that he'd fall in love with her, given half a chance. Mostly because he'd never fallen out of love with her.

CHAPTER NINE

MITCH FOLLOWED the rich scent of coffee to the kitchen. It was early, just after six, but Darcy was up, dressed and looking like a million bucks. He felt a stir, an awareness, a desire that had clearly simmered all night.

She smiled at him, but it turned into a yawn.

"Didn't sleep well?" He filled a mug with the steaming brew and worked hard at making sure he sounded casual. As if he woke up to see her each morning.

"Oh, I got a few hours," she said, yawning again.

"Is that normal?"

She shook her head, causing her dark hair to shimmer in the light streaming in the window. "I'm a hell of a sleeper. I've considered going pro."

"So what happened last night?"

She got her mug and sat at the table. Then she crossed her legs. Her foot jiggled nervously, but he doubted she was aware of that.

He sat, too, and sipped his coffee. It was perfect. *She was perfect.*

"I've made a decision."

He put his cup down.

"I'm firing you as my doctor."

The relief that flooded through him was his first

indication of how much he'd wanted her to say just that.

"It's not that I think you're—"

"I understand," he said, interrupting her bid to reassure him. "Are you still planning to have the AI?"

She nodded, but there was some hesitance, he thought. Or maybe not.

"I'll refer you to Terry Miller. She's an excellent doctor. You'll like her. And if you have any questions or any doubts, you come to me, okay?"

This time when she nodded, there was no reservation. In fact, she looked relieved.

"Darcy?"

"Hmm?"

"It's because of last night, right?"

She didn't answer him right away. She drank more coffee, and her foot kicked into high gear as she pushed her hair behind her left ear. "I'm not sure," she said. "I mean, I'm not sure about much of anything at the moment. I've made too many big decisions in too short a time. I just need to think for a while. Once I get into my house and the press forgets about me, things will be different."

She hadn't said anything about him. About them. Perhaps last night hadn't meant anything. But her nervousness alone told him it did. She'd been knocked for a loop by the strength of her desire, just as he had. She didn't want to talk about it, and he wasn't sure he did, either. "So what's on the agenda for today?"

"I'm going to call Hank. He's my manager. He'll help with the press. I'm going to have him announce my retirement. It'll cause a minor flurry, but then, hopefully, I'll be left alone."

"Are you going to talk about the baby?"

She shook her head. "No. Not yet. Maybe not ever."

"I think people might have already guessed."

"Yeah, I know. But I don't have to confirm it." She got up and poured herself some more coffee, even though she hadn't finished half a cup. "Last night," she said as she sat down again, "I was thinking about the baby and all. At some point, the child is going to be able to read. And if the fact that I was artificially inseminated is in the papers, she's bound to have questions."

"So tell her about it before that."

"Seriously?"

He nodded. "I'll introduce you to my neighbor. Her little boy was conceived that way, and she's quite willing to talk about it. He's known about his birth for a long time, and he seems to have accepted the facts with no trouble."

"Adam?"

"You know him?"

"I'm sorry. I forgot to tell you. He came by yesterday. You were supposed to help him with his math."

Mitch closed his eyes for a moment, cursing himself silently. "I forgot."

"It's okay. I helped him."

"You did?"

"He's great."

"Yeah. He is. He's sharp, too. Thank you."

"Was she inseminated at Maitland?"

"Yes. I was Charlotte's doctor. In fact, she found her town house after coming to visit me with Adam."

"Is there...you know, more than a doctor-patient thing going on with you two?"

"No," he said quickly. "No. I haven't really dated much. Not since my wife passed away."

Darcy studied his face as she sipped coffee. He didn't seem upset at the mention of his wife. She'd learned the details of his marriage and his wife's death from Beth and Abby. But she didn't get the feeling that Mitch wanted to discuss it. She'd take a step back, for now. Later, she'd ask about it. When... If... "So when did Charlotte tell him?"

"As soon as he was old enough to start asking questions about families. I think she has some read-along books that are about special kids like Adam."

"I'd like to meet her."

"And you should. I'm a big proponent of AI. It's made all the difference in many people's lives. But you need to think it over very carefully. Do as much research as possible. I know there's a great deal of information on the Internet, although be careful, because it's not always accurate."

"I'm not planning on rushing this. Of course, I don't want to wait too much longer. I'm thirty-four, and the old biological clock is ringing pretty loudly."

"May I ask— Never mind. It's none of my business."

"What?"

"It doesn't matter."

"Mitch," she said in her sternest voice.

"Okay, okay. I just wondered why you've decided to go this route. You could—"

"Have any man." She finished the sentence for him, having heard it about a thousand times.

He nodded. She looked at him for a while, debating how much to tell him. God, he was handsome. Not in the traditional sense, but he appealed to her in a way she could hardly explain. Just looking at him made her feel better. Perhaps it was because she felt safe with him. Safe that he wasn't after her for her money or her fame.

"Are you hungry?" she asked.

He shrugged, but he didn't push her to answer his question. She got up and pulled a carton of eggs from the fridge, along with butter and bread and jelly. She kept herself busy for the next few minutes whipping up an omelet. It would have been better with mushrooms and tomatoes, but there weren't any in the fridge.

When she saw Mitch look at his watch, she realized she'd procrastinated as long as she could. After lowering the flame under the omelet pan, she faced him. "Despite what you might think from the newspapers, being a model is a very lousy way to meet men."

He grinned. "Why don't I believe you?"

"Okay, so you meet a lot of men. Let me rephrase. It's a lousy way to meet good men."

"By that, I take it you mean men who weren't like your ex-husband?"

"Yes. And men who aren't into cocaine as a hobby. Or who don't look at women as really expensive accessories to go along with their Manhattan penthouses and Mercedes limousines."

"All of them were that bad?"

"Probably not. But I wasn't around one place long enough to separate the wheat from the chaff. All I know is, modeling, at least the way I did it, was not a healthy environment. It was a small pond filled with large sharks, and from the first time I stepped out onto a runway, I felt like bait.''

''Why didn't you quit before?''

She turned back to the eggs. ''It's complicated. Partly because of the money. Frankly, it's obscene. And I had a goal. To be out of the business, in a real home with a husband and child, by the time I was thirty-five. As the years went on, I amended the goal. I took out the husband. And that's why I'm here.''

She flipped the cooked omelet onto a plate, grabbed two forks then went back to the table and put the eggs between them.

He took a bite, and his eyes widened with pleasure. She felt inordinately pleased.

''All I want,'' she went on, ''is a normal life. PTA meetings, car pools, gardens, grocery shopping. And you know what else? I want to eat.''

''What do you mean?''

''I've been on a diet for sixteen years. I'm too thin, and I don't remember what it's like to eat until I'm full. The odd thing is, I'm not having such an easy time of it. I've tried to pig out, I really have, but I guess it's too soon. I've been afraid of food so long, I don't know how to see it as a friend.''

''It'll happen.''

She smiled. ''Yeah, and I'll end up huge. But I don't care. A woman I know, a really successful model, had a baby not long ago. She couldn't breast-feed. She didn't eat enough to supply milk to her son. I thought that was awful.''

He ate for a while in silence, and she tried to match his pace, but it wasn't going to happen. Still, she did eat her half. And then she took a piece of bread, spread it thickly with butter and jam and ate every bite.

"Well done," Mitch said.

She bowed her head, pleased with the tiny victory.

He started to get up but paused. "Do you remember that night in the park? That summer night when we sat on the swings?"

The memory came back, carrying a whole bushel of feelings with it. "Yeah. I do."

"You said you wanted a family. Two kids, maybe three. A dog, a cat. A nice guy. A two-story house with a swimming pool in the back yard."

"And I also said I wanted to be a science teacher."

"That's right."

"You wanted to be a doctor."

"I sure did."

"It's taken a lot longer than I ever dreamed." She finished the last small bite of omelet, then took the plate to the sink. "But at least I'm here. And I'm not going to let some stupid tabloid journalist ruin it for me."

He came over to her and touched her shoulder. "I'm still sorry," he said. "I'd like to make this easier for you, not harder."

When she turned, he was closer than she expected. Close like last night. Her heart pounded as she thought of what had almost happened. He'd kept her awake for hours. Reliving the feel of his body against hers, wanting more, wanting him. He'd filled her head with fantasies, of love rekindled, of happily ever after, even though she knew it was a foolish hope.

She didn't know a lot about Mitch, but she did

know about his wife. About her death and how he'd mourned. Was still mourning.

It was too soon to tell if her coming back would change anything. If she could be his answer, and he could be hers. It might be all wrong. Or exactly right. No point in rushing things. Or hoping too hard.

He kissed her cheek, then she felt him take a deep breath. "I've got to get to work," he whispered.

"I know. Go."

"I don't want to leave you."

"I'll be fine."

His hand moved down her arm slowly, making her shiver with the contact. "Call me if you need anything."

She nodded.

He broke away and went to the door to the garage. Just before he walked out, he stopped at the counter. She'd left the Polaroid of them at the science fair lying there, meaning to ask him about it. He turned to her with a puzzled look. A hurt look.

"What's wrong?"

He shook his head.

"Mitch, what is it?"

"I was just wondering why you left so suddenly all those years ago. I didn't get to say goodbye."

She opened her mouth, stunned at his obvious earnestness. Something was dreadfully wrong. She had the awful feeling her mother was in the middle of it.

"We'll talk about it later. I'm late as it is."

She nodded, but her mind had gone to those horrible last days before she'd left for New York. What had her mother done?

Long minutes later she still stood at the counter,

her gaze on the photo. She remembered it being taken. She remembered how she'd felt when Mitch touched her back. How the sensation had been so intense. She'd been scared to death. Who was she kidding? She was still scared to death.

THE GUN FELT GOOD in his hand. Petey hefted the .357 Magnum, admiring the clean lines and the awesome power. He'd use it soon. Very soon. But first he had to make sure there was no way he would get caught.

He turned the weapon and examined his handiwork. There was no sign of a serial number left. It was spit-polished and lick-boot clean. Janelle had gotten the gun—how, he didn't know and didn't care. But she hadn't known where the serial number was, let alone that they had to sand it off.

Something wasn't right there. The gun, the timing, the whole setup. It didn't feel smooth, that's what it was. It felt...

She'd double-cross him. He knew it as well as he knew his own face. The woman would double-cross him if it came down to that. So it wouldn't come down to that. He'd make damn sure. The payoff was too sweet. He'd be set up for the rest of his life, Janelle or no Janelle.

She wanted him to off Lacy after the gala. He didn't understand why. She didn't even try to explain. Instead, she'd looked at him like he was a moron.

Well, surprise, Janelle. He'd decide when and how. Not her. He'd decide, and then he'd do what he needed to do. Right now, he had to sit tight and watch for Lacy to leave Austin Eats.

He slipped the gun under the front seat, then checked the street again. His car was parked down the block, but he'd know when she left. She had to walk past him. No other way for her to get home.

So tonight, he'd follow her. He wouldn't do anything. Well, maybe...

He'd follow her, and then he'd come up with a plan. A friggin' doozy of a plan.

Janelle would look at him different after this. She wouldn't be so damn bitchy all the time. And if she still was? Adios.

Yeah. Adios.

CHAPTER TEN

MITCH SHUT THE DOOR to his office. It was almost one, and this was the first time he'd been able to sit down since he'd arrived. It was one of those days when every patient took longer than anticipated, and Murphy's Law struck at every turn.

He'd have to start again in half an hour, which didn't leave him much time to eat lunch. Thankfully, his secretary had ordered sandwiches, which should be arriving at any moment.

All he wanted to do was relax. He turned his chair toward the window and leaned back, closing his eyes, appreciating the warmth on his face.

His thoughts turned to Darcy. Which didn't help with the relaxation. She'd looked stunned when he'd brought up her abrupt departure. Why? Surely she remembered that she'd left without a word.

The day he'd discovered she'd gone was branded in his memory. It had been a particularly beautiful day. April. Just a few short months till graduation. He'd ridden over on the bike he'd gotten for his birthday, and he'd stashed an envelope filled with licorice Necco wafers in his shirt pocket, because Darcy liked them so much.

He'd had to ring the doorbell four times, and when Mrs. Taylor opened the door, she'd seemed annoyed at him. Her face had gone red when he'd asked if Darcy was ready for their study date.

At the time, he'd been so crushed, he hadn't stopped to think about Mrs. Taylor. Could she have sent Darcy away? Could that be it? Had her mother sent her to New York without her consent?

He pictured Darcy as she'd looked this morning. So taken aback, so confused. That had to be the real story. But if it were, why hadn't Darcy said goodbye? Or explained the situation to him? Surely there had been more than a few hours' notice.

He turned and reached for the telephone, but just as his hand touched the receiver, there was a knock on his door. "Come in."

His secretary, Eleanor, entered with lunch and a soda. She puttered for a moment, pulling out his napkin, opening the soda...all the things she did at home for her three-year-old. Mitch was used to her fussing. He'd told her over and over that it wasn't necessary, but finally, he'd given up. Bringing it to her attention only embarrassed her.

"You have two new appointments for today," Eleanor said as she sat in the guest chair. "Mr. and Mrs. Todd want to come by."

That wasn't going to be fun. Mrs. Todd had suffered a miscarriage, her fourth. Mitchell wasn't at all sure she could ever carry a baby to term. He knew they were heartbroken about it and searching for a miracle he didn't have.

"And a young man by the name of Adam has asked for an appointment at three-thirty, after school lets out."

"Pardon me?"

"He said he's your neighbor." Eleanor smiled. She looked at him with her friendly eyes, prodding him silently to explain, please.

"Yeah, it's true. He is my neighbor. And he met Darcy yesterday."

"Ah," she said. "That explains it."

"How?"

"He met Darcy. It wouldn't surprise me a bit if he's fallen in love with her. I think he's coming to ask if he can see her again."

"He's nine."

Eleanor shrugged, then folded her hands on her lap, so prim and proper she looked like someone's benevolent aunt. No one would ever guess that on the weekends she taught self-defense at retirement homes, and that she could take down a two-hundred-pound man in about two seconds flat. "It doesn't matter that he's nine. Love comes whenever it comes, and it's just as real at nine as it is at thirty-nine."

"It still doesn't make sense that he's coming to see me."

"Perhaps I'm wrong," she said.

But he knew that tone. She meant she was right, and he'd have to admit it before she'd let it alone.

"Now, eat your sandwich. You've only got fifteen minutes before Mrs. Gardner."

He nodded, but didn't reach for his food. He was thinking about Adam. About him falling in love with Darcy. It was probably true. Mitch had fallen for her at eight. He hadn't known it until he was about fifteen, but all the signs were there years before that. The quickening of his heart whenever he saw her. The goofy grin he got when she said something nice. Hell, he'd even traded his peanut butter sandwiches for her tuna fish, and he hated tuna fish.

He'd probably fallen for her the first time he'd laid eyes on her. Not like with Angela. He'd appreciated Angela for her subtle wit, for her softness and her compassion. He'd felt at peace with her, almost always.

With Darcy, there was no peace. It was all sound and fury and desperation. He'd loved her because she was smarter than him, could run faster, could hit harder. She left him tongue-tied and dazed. No, there was no peace with Darcy. There still wasn't.

Which convinced him more than anything else that what he had on his hands was a case of arrested development. Around her, he was fifteen. But if he just gave it a little time, he'd calm down and things would be right again.

He looked up to find his office empty, the door closed. He hadn't heard Eleanor leave. And he hadn't eaten his sandwich. When he glanced at his watch, he saw that ten minutes had gone by. That was like old times, too. He'd wasted many a day, and too many nights, thinking about Darcy Taylor. It was time for him to put away his childish attitudes. He needed to get to know the Darcy Taylor of today and banish the girl he'd once loved.

"I NEED YOUR HELP."

"So, what's new?" Hank asked, his voice a little dim over the cellular phone.

Darcy smiled as she settled into the leather chair in Mitch's living room. "Hey, *I'm* not the one who got into a fistfight at the Met."

"I won't dignify that with a reply."

"Dignify, my patootie. You were scandalous."

She heard him sigh. "Yeah, I was. It was great. So what can I do to help you, fair maiden?"

"They're on to me."

Hank sighed. "Oh, crap."

"Oh, crap, indeed. They were swarming at the house yesterday. I couldn't even get in."

"So that's why you didn't answer my calls."

"I'm staying at a friend's house. I'm afraid to walk outside."

"Darcy, my love, did you really think you could keep this private? Quitting Avelon in the middle of your contract, moving to Texas of all places? Having a child all by your lonesome?"

"No." She swung her leg over the arm of the chair and snuggled down. "I didn't believe it, really. I just thought I'd have more time."

"I wish you could have had more time, too," Hank said, his voice fading then coming back. "What cretin let the cat out of the bag?"

She felt her cheeks heat, which surprised her. The urge to come to Mitch's defense surprised her even more. "Someone from Maitland Maternity. It's not important."

There was a long pause. Too long. As if Hank was jumping to conclusions or something.

"Hello?"

"I'm here," he said. "And I think it would be best if we had a little press conference."

"No."

"Yes."

"I *hate* that."

"I know, love. But they'll never stop. You know that as well as I do. They'll hound it out of you, and worse, they'll bungle it. The tabloids will still lie about it, but this way you're giving a nod to the legitimate press, who, I should remind you, have been very good to you."

She closed her eyes, not wanting to admit that Hank was right. She could imagine the hoopla that would erupt when the press got wind of her baby plans. "Listen, I'm not sure I want to say anything about the baby yet."

"You don't think they'll find out?"

"No. Especially if I don't go through with it."

"What?"

"Yet. If I don't go through with it *yet*."

"That's not what you said."

"I know."

"So, you want to tell me what's going on?"

She sighed. "I'm not sure myself."

"I'm here if you need to talk."

"I know. Thank you."

"It's my job. What's also my job is to set up the press conference. The baby issue won't be on the agenda."

"Good. And I don't want Maitland Maternity to be brought into this, either. They've had enough trouble lately."

"They got you into this mess."

"No, they didn't. I got here on my own power."

Another pause. She could picture him pulling his earlobe, the way he always did when he was nervous. "Who are you staying with, Darcy?"

"An old friend. He's a doctor at Maitland. Which can explain why I visited there."

"Maitland," he said, drawing the word out slowly. "Mitchell Maitland. Wasn't he the boy that—"

"Yes. But that was a long time ago."

"And yet, there you are."

"I guess you can go home again," she said, more brightly than she felt. "At least, I think so."

"I hope you know what you're doing."

She laughed. "Not a clue. I'm just taking one step at a time and praying it comes out all right."

"I'll do my part. What's the number there?"

She had to get Mitch's number out of her purse, and when that was done, Hank talked for a few minutes more about the press situation, but she wasn't really listening. Her thoughts had gone to Mitch. To what he'd said this morning. Distracted, she said goodbye to her manager, then went into the kitchen. The picture was on the table.

What a day that had been. How perfect her world had seemed.

She didn't want to think about that now. It was too easy to get herself in a lather. But what was she going to do with herself? A run was what she needed. To get out and use her muscles and get her heart pumping. The idea appealed so much, she hurried to her room, changed into running gear, then got her sunglasses and hat. She certainly didn't need to be spotted jogging near Mitchell's place.

Although what did it matter? No one knew about her past with Mitch. And even if they did, why would they care? He was just a boy she'd known in school.

A boy she'd loved. Who'd accepted her unconditionally. Who'd made losing her father bearable.

She flushed as she remembered how her body had reacted to his touch. Something was going on between them. She needed time to discover what.

It wasn't until she'd run three blocks that she realized she'd told Hank the truth—she wasn't sure about the baby anymore. Not that she didn't want a baby. That hadn't changed. But she wasn't sure how the baby was going to be conceived. Perhaps she'd come home to find the baby a daddy?

MITCH GOT the box of tissues he kept by his desk and handed it to Craig Todd. He and his wife, Kathy, were both crying. Mitch wished there was something he could do to comfort them. They wanted a child so badly.

Craig cleared his throat, and Mitch could see him struggle to gain his composure. "What about using donor sperm?"

Mitch shook his head. "I'm sorry. The problem isn't with the sperm." He didn't want to say it again. Kathy was too shattered to hear once more that it was her own body that had betrayed her. That her uterus wasn't capable of carrying a child to term.

Craig nodded. Kathy wiped her eyes, then reached out so her husband could take her hand. They were young. Twenty-six. Married for three years, and one of the happiest couples he'd ever met. They'd had such hope.

"There is adoption," Mitch offered.

Kathy shook her head. "No. Not yet. Not yet. I just keep thinking…"

"Of course." Mitch came around his desk and leaned against it. "You take all the time you need. Whatever your decision, I'll be here to help."

"Thanks, Dr. Maitland. I mean it." Craig stood up and shook his hand. "You've been great."

"I just wish..."

Craig turned abruptly, and Mitch realized he should leave the couple to their mourning. It was a loss, as real as any other, not to be able to conceive. It could break up a marriage. It could destroy a woman's confidence. He knew full well that procreation was the strongest biological urge of all.

But he also knew that there were so many unwanted children, that a couple like the Todds could end up with a large family, despite her infertility.

Kathy was weeping harder. Mitch headed for his office door. "I need to see my nurse," he said. "You two take all the time you need. I won't be back soon."

Craig nodded, his arms were around his wife's shoulders, and Mitch slipped out the door and closed it behind him. He didn't really need to see his nurse. His appointments were done for the day, except for one. Adam.

Mitch went to the reception desk and peered over the counter. Sure enough, his young neighbor sat in the biggest of the waiting room chairs, his feet dangling as he read the latest copy of *Highlights*. Mitch had checked with Charlotte about Adam's appointment, but she had no idea what it was about. Darcy, probably. But he'd soon find out.

Mitch walked into the reception area, and Adam put the magazine down then climbed off the chair.

When he met Mitch's gaze, his eyes were serious, and so was his posture. Mitch held out his hand, and after a second, Adam grabbed it and gave him a hell of a shake.

"Adam, I've got a proposition for you."

"Huh?"

Mitch smiled at him and crouched down to his eye level. "Some nice people are in my office, and I'd hate to kick them out. How about you and I go across the street to the diner. We can sit at a private table and talk there."

Adam didn't leap at the offer.

"It will be just as good as being in my office," Mitch reassured him. "And just as confidential."

"Okay."

"Good. Because I'm in the mood for a root beer float."

That got Adam's attention. But he didn't talk all the way out of the clinic or across the street, which was unusual for him. Normally Mitch could hardly get a word in edgewise.

Just as they reached the door to Austin Eats, Mitch caught a glimpse of Connor O'Hara. Their eyes met for a second, then Connor slipped around the corner before Mitch could say hello. Odd. But it was for the best. This was Adam's hour.

Inside, Mitch had Shelby seat them at the most isolated table, and Adam and he ordered floats.

"Dr. Maitland?"

Mitch fought a grin. If Adam was calling him Dr. Maitland, then this was serious, indeed.

"I was wondering…"

"Yes?"

"I've been thinking. I know all the other kids in my class have fathers. And Mom keeps telling me that I'm special and that I have all the family I need. But I must have a father, right? I mean, Mom couldn't have done it all herself."

"No, she couldn't have."

He nodded, dislodging a thatch of hair that dangled over his forehead.

"I saw this show on the Discovery channel. They said how an egg and a sperm have to do something together. I wasn't exactly sure, 'cause my mom called me to take out the garbage in the middle, but I was pretty sure it took a father and a mother. So, what I was wondering... Who is my father?"

Mitch cursed silently as he smiled at the boy. He reached into his coat pocket and pulled out his cell phone. "Adam, can you wait just one second? I forgot an important phone call, but when I get back, we'll talk about your questions."

Adam nodded.

Mitch bolted out of his chair and headed toward Shelby. He asked her to bring Adam a piece of apple pie along with the float. That would keep him busy for a few minutes. Then he dialed Charlotte's house, praying she was home.

She answered on the second ring.

"Charlotte, thank God."

"What's wrong?"

"Nothing. Everything's fine. Adam's here with me. I found out what his appointment was about."

"What?"

"He wants to know who his father is."

She didn't answer him for a while. He turned and

nodded at Shelby, who was just putting Adam's slice of pie down.

"Oh, dear. I'm sorry he's put you in such an awkward position."

"It's okay. But I didn't want to overstep. If you want to come down…"

"No. I think he asked to see you because he needs to hear this from someone he trusts. Someone who's not his mother."

"I was under the impression you'd told him about the AI."

"I have. I didn't go into detail."

"Ah."

"So, if you wouldn't mind?"

"No, not at all. Do you want me to tell him everything?"

"Yes. If he's old enough to ask, he's old enough to know. But the most important thing is to tell him how much I love him."

"That won't be a problem."

"Thanks, Mitch. Really. Oh, and Mitch?"

"Yes?"

"Is it true you have a supermodel living in your house?"

Mitch coughed. "It's a little hard to explain."

"I didn't mean to pry."

"You're not. I'll tell you all about it when I bring Adam home. But, Charlotte, do me a favor. Don't mention her to anyone, okay?"

"Oops."

"Oops?"

"I kind of told my Junior League friends."

"And how many friends would that be?"

"About fifty."

"Oops."

"You take care of Adam. I'll go next door and warn your friend."

"We'll be home soon," he said. He clicked his phone shut and looked at Adam eating pie. He couldn't short-change the boy. Not as important as this talk was. But damn, he wished he could go home to be with Darcy. She never should have come back to Austin. Since she'd met him, everything had gone wrong. She should probably leave town and not come back.

But he hoped she wouldn't. He didn't want her to leave. Not yet.

CHAPTER ELEVEN

SHE FELT GOOD. Strong. Even with the sweat, and her breathing becoming more and more strained. Running always got her centered. She didn't run just to keep in shape. She ran so she could be alone. Inevitably, if she concentrated, she'd hit the zone, and that's when the crazies faded and rational thought took over.

Of course she would tell the press she'd quit modeling. And of course she wouldn't say anything about wanting a child. It wasn't going to be so bad. She'd make jokes, and Hank would sidestep any troubling questions. She'd talk about her friendship with the Maitlands, how they'd been there for her all during her childhood. She'd smile and let them take their pictures, and then they would go away.

That was the way it had to be for now. Later, they wouldn't come at all, but for now, it was better to ride the horse in the direction it was going. The press might be able to take her photograph, but they couldn't take anything real from her.

Now that she'd resigned herself to a press conference, her thoughts turned to Mitch as she rounded the corner. The streets, tree-lined and peaceful, captured her attention for a moment. The lovely large houses all seemed asleep, and she wondered about the people inside them. Were they happy? Did they realize how lucky they were?

Mitch. Once again, his name and his image came to her. It was something of a shock to realize the pictures in her head had changed. For so many years, she'd imagined him as the boy he used to be. Now she saw him as a man.

She knew so much about him, up to a point, and then his life became a mystery. She could guess what medical school had been like, but she had no idea about his courtship and marriage.

Those were the years she hadn't kept in touch with Beth, years spent mostly in Europe. Darcy hadn't even known Mitch had gotten married. Or that his wife had died a year later.

How hard that must have been for him. So tragic. So traumatic. Did it still haunt him? Was Angela with him every day in his heart?

It was horrible, something she felt terribly guilty about, but she was jealous of Angela. It would have been so great to have gone to college with Mitch. Medical school had been right up there when she dreamed of the future. With Mitch there, the competition would have been fierce. She would have had to be on her toes every single day. But it would have been so much fun.

Instead, she'd been in Milan, which sounded great. Unfortunately, it wasn't, except for the sight-seeing, which she hardly got to do. It was in Milan that her career had really taken off. That first cover of Italian *Vogue*. The first Versace show.

God, how lonely she'd been. How she'd dreamed of home. Of Mitch. All she'd wanted was to run away, but there was always her mother and always the guilt.

But not anymore. She wasn't going to live her life for anyone else. Well, except her children. God, she hoped there were lots. A whole house full.

Mitch would be an incredible daddy. His generous heart, his even temperament, his brains and his sense of humor were everything she'd looked for in a husband. She hadn't found it anywhere, of course.

It had only just occurred to her that Mitch had been her benchmark. Every man tried to measure up. None of them had come close.

So why was she looking for someone *like* Mitch when she could have Mitch?

She turned the corner and pumped up the speed for the last hundred yards. By the time she stopped, she could hardly breathe. Panting, walking to cool down her muscles, she realized how presumptuous it was to assume she could have Mitch. Such *supermodel* thinking. Such nonsense.

But wanting Mitch wasn't nonsense. Now all she had to do was figure out how to go about getting him.

MITCH SIPPED his coffee, his gaze on his young visitor. Adam had finished his pie, and now he shifted nervously on his chair, gearing himself up to ask the tough questions.

"The thing is," he said, "I know I have a different kind of family. But, I mean, I do have a father, right?"

"Yes, you do."

"So, um, who is he?"

"That's not an easy question to answer. Your

mother and he never met. She found out a lot about him. What he looked like, how he'd done in school, things like that. But they never met.''

Adam's face was a picture of confusion. No wonder. Artificial insemination was a tough concept for adults, let alone nine-year-olds.

''You see, Adam, when your mother came to see me for the first time, she told me that more than anything in the whole world, she wanted a baby. Someone she could love her whole life long. The problem was, she wasn't married, and she wasn't in love with anyone. But that didn't stop her from wanting a child.''

Adam nodded solemnly.

''The reason she came to see me is that I'm a fertility specialist. That means I try to help when a couple or an individual wants to conceive, but can't—for whatever reason.''

Adam's hands went to his lap, and his cheeks became infused with pink. ''Are you...?''

Mitch grinned. ''No. I'm just the doctor. Do you know how babies are made?''

''We learned about it in health. The sperms and the eggs and stuff.''

''Right. What I do is help that to happen. It's a little complicated, but in the end, what happens is that a woman like your mother can have a child, and they can be a family together.''

''So we don't know my father's name?''

Mitch sipped coffee, more to take a moment to compose himself than because he was thirsty. This wasn't easy. Adam clearly wanted a father. A real, flesh-and-blood person to be in his life. But that was something he couldn't have. Under the terms of the agreement, the donor was confidential, except for medical records. "No, Adam. We don't. But we do know that he wanted to give women, a woman like your mom, a chance to have a family. So right there we know he was a good man, right?"

"I guess." He sighed. "I was just hoping…" He shrugged.

"I know. But the thing to remember is how much your mother loves you. How you came to be because she wanted you so very much."

"Yeah. Okay. I guess." His gaze darted to Mitch, then skittered to the table. "Is Darcy still at your house?"

Mitch had wondered when that was going to come up. "Yes, she is. But she won't be there for long."

"She's pretty."

"Very."

"And she sure knows math."

"Tell me about it. She always got better grades than me in school."

Eyes animated, elbows on the table, Adam leaned forward. "I know. She told me. She said she used to clean your clock."

Mitch grinned. "She did, did she? Well, I don't know about that."

"She said you'd deny it. She said—" He stopped short, his cheeks reddening again.

"I can just imagine what she said."

Adam got down from his chair. "I'd better get going. I don't want to be late for dinner."

"Want a ride home?"

"Sure."

"Okay. Maybe we can talk some more. If you want to."

"I don't want to."

"Fair enough." Mitch put his money on the table, then stood to usher Adam to the door. "Let's go get the car, shall we?"

The boy led the way across the street, then followed Mitch to his car. True to his word, he didn't talk anymore. But his face telegraphed what he was thinking about. It wasn't his father. It was a tall beauty who'd kicked Mitch's butt in chemistry. Who'd been his study partner and his friend. Who'd been his first love. Maybe his only love.

But now wasn't the time to get swept away with thoughts of Darcy, Mitch chided himself. He had a young man in his care. Full of questions and confusion. Searching for answers. Maybe Mitch couldn't answer all his questions, but he could be there for Adam. It wouldn't be as good as having a real dad, of course. But it was something.

He looked over. Adam, with his dark hair, his gangly arms and legs, was such a great kid. It wasn't hard to imagine having a boy like him. Being a real father.

Darcy shouldn't have the artificial insemination. The thought stopped him in his tracks. Stopped him cold. It wasn't his business. He was nothing to her but an old friend. And yet...

"Come on, Adam. Let's go see if Darcy is home now."

THE AROMA in the kitchen was so heavenly, Darcy was tempted to increase the oven temperature so the chicken would be done sooner. But she held back. She wanted everything to be perfect tonight.

She eyed the table, set with linen napkins, candles and flowers picked from Mitch's yard. The salad was made and in the fridge, as was the balsamic vinaigrette. The potatoes would be done at the same time as the roast chicken, and the carrots were cooking very slowly on the stove. The only thing left to do was finish making dessert, a steamed custard laced with Grand Marnier.

Charlotte had been a peach to do all the shopping. Well, to send in the order. It seemed while Darcy had been busy on the runways in Milan and Paris, grocery shopping had gone through some changes. Now, all one had to do was go on-line, click on the products and voilà—someone would deliver them straight to the door. Heavens. It boggled the mind. It also made her curious to do some financial research on this approach to domestic bliss.

She cracked two more eggs, separated the yolks and added them to the sugar, milk and vanilla in the silver bowl. Then she stirred, checked the recipe once more, added the liqueur and poured the mixture into ramekins. The water in the bain marie came to a steaming simmer, and a moment later, she put the lid on the pot.

This was so cool. Cooking dinner. Listening to Enya sing about the Oronoco flow. Waiting breathlessly for the sound of the garage door to open.

For the first time in God knew how long, she felt *real*. The wonder of it was that she hadn't felt this way for years. Not since she'd left here. Not since Mitch.

She'd felt like a walking mannequin, an ordinary girl in a gorgeous Halloween costume that she couldn't take off. She'd felt like a thing, not a person.

She'd never belonged in that world.

But now, if she played her cards right, she could have what she truly wanted. A home. A child. And perhaps...

It was getting late, and she wanted to take a quick shower before Mitch got home. She wanted to talk to him tonight. Her conversation with Charlotte had been eye-opening, and she had some questions for Mitch about AI. But mostly, she wanted to talk to him about the missing years. To understand his feelings for his wife.

Dinner would be ready in half an hour, and she would be, too. As she headed toward the guest room, she felt exhilarated. Nervous. Perhaps she was setting herself up, being this excited about the evening. Maybe nothing at all would happen. Her expectations had gotten her into trouble before.

But somehow she felt she was right about this. That tonight, she would discover if she really knew Mitch—if he was anything like the man she thought he was.

"GOOD NIGHT."

Sara waved at Mary Jane as she headed out the back door of the diner. But her smile faded the moment she was out of her friend's view. Tonight had been tough. Not just the headache, although that had been bad enough to make her want to scream, but the tension in her gut. The way she felt as if someone was watching her. The way she jumped at the least little thing.

She still couldn't believe what had happened this afternoon. For heaven's sake, she knew the sound of a car backfiring. It wasn't as if she believed it was a gunshot or anything. And she'd dropped two fully prepared plates.

Shelby had been great about it, but it had been embarrassing all the same.

If only she could remember. Anything. Anything important. The doctor had said how lucky she was that she could read and write. That she had the right words for objects, and that her short-term memory was completely intact.

It could have been so much worse.

She headed down the deserted street, moving from darkness to lamplight every few steps. The feeling came back, the one she had for days. As if she had a target over the small of her back, just waiting for someone to pick her off.

She liked to think someone was looking for her. Someone who cared for her. A husband? A child? What if there was a life out there, with neighbors and dogs and PTA meetings?

She didn't like to think of the alternative. What if the memory loss was her way of hiding from the past? From something terrible? Her dreams were so bad sometimes. But when she woke up, she couldn't remember what had scared her so.

Once she reached the corner, she waited for a gold Lexus to pass, then she crossed the street. It was shameful to be thinking such negative thoughts. Life was good here. Strange, but good. She would be sorry to leave the diner. If she did have someone out there, she hoped it was someone kind. She couldn't take it if she'd done something bad. Something shameful.

She reached the next corner, and the rooming house was just across the street. She stepped down from the curb, then noticed a car at full speed toward her.

A gold Lexus.

Her hackles rose, and the tension in her stomach twisted like a knife. That car wasn't just traveling down the street, it was headed right for her!

Seconds before the front bumper would have hit her, she leaped back, falling on the grass next to the bus stop. Her hands went out to break the fall, and her purse flew from her grasp.

Pain hit both her shoulders as she landed, and the wind was knocked out of her. For a terrifying second, she thought the car was going to hit her, but it veered left, then sped off with a squeal of tires that shattered the night.

She tried to breathe, but as the seconds ticked by and she couldn't catch her breath, the panic rose unbearably. Then something inside her throat unlocked, and sweet night air filled her lungs.

It was only then that she started shaking.

It was hardly paranoia when someone really *was* out to get you.

CHARLOTTE MET THEM in Mitch's driveway. She smiled widely the moment her gaze landed on her son. Mitch didn't open the garage door. He parked the car and let Adam out. Charlotte gave him a tight hug. "You okay, kiddo?"

"Sure. What's for dinner?"

She laughed, signaling her relief to Mitch with a short shake of her head. "Hot dogs."

"Cool!" He turned to Mitch and gave him a half wave before he ran across the yard and into his house.

Charlotte came to the car window. "How'd it go?"

"Fine. He's a good kid."

"What did you tell him about his father?"

"The truth. That we don't know who he is. I think he understood."

"Is he upset?"

"Not that I could see. I wouldn't worry about it, Charlotte. He's curious. It's as natural as breathing."

Her smile faded, and she fiddled with her gold chain necklace. She was a nice-looking woman, and there had been a time when he'd thought about taking their relationship in a different direction. But there was no spark between them. He hadn't been completely convinced about that until this moment. All he wanted to do was go in and see Darcy. To look at her and know she was real, and really in his home. In his life.

"I know I didn't make a mistake," Charlotte said. "But sometimes..."

"We all have challenges," he said, hoping he could reassure her. "And every parent in the world wonders if they're doing it right."

"I suppose so."

"Just go on the way you are. Don't worry about it. He's gonna be fine, and so are you."

She stepped back. "Thanks, Mitch. I owe you one."

"No, you don't."

"Actually, you're right. I don't. I gave your guest a hand today, so that makes us even."

He looked at the front door, then at Charlotte. "Is she okay?"

"Oh, sure. My God, she's gorgeous. It would be so easy to hate her. But she's really nice. Damn it. And Adam says she has brains. If you ask me, that's pretty damn rude."

"I'll tell her you think so."

"Don't you dare! I like her. She was great about me opening my big mouth. She says she's going to have a press conference anyway, so it didn't make a difference."

"A press conference?"

"Yeah. To announce her retirement and all. And then I went shopping. Not physically, of course. I don't do shopping like that anymore. But I got everything delivered. Filled the fridge with food. Damn nice of me, huh?"

He laughed. Charlotte had such a peculiar sense of humor. One he liked a lot. "Yes, damn nice of you."

"Now go on inside. She's been cooking all afternoon. Make a fuss."

He pushed the garage door opener, and by the time he looked at Charlotte, she'd crossed into her yard. Mitch put the car in gear. He was suddenly thirsty. Warm. Nervous. It was ridiculous. A grown man shouldn't be this tense about walking into his own house.

But who was he kidding? Around Darcy, he was fifteen again. At least on the inside. Fifteen, and out of control.

Thank God he had a medical book to carry.

CHAPTER TWELVE

HAVING JUST LIT the second candle, Darcy went to blow out her match. Right then the door opened. She was about to say something welcoming when the heat of the flame burned her finger, and she shook her hand wildly to get rid of the match. It fell to the floor—out, but the damage was done. Her picture-perfect scenario had been spoiled.

"Are you all right?"

She nodded. "That's what I get for playing with fire."

Mitch put his book on the counter then took her hand in his, examining her wound. Even though it hurt, it wasn't visible to the naked eye. Still, Mitch looked terribly concerned, which was terribly sweet.

"I think I'll live," she said.

"Ice is good for this sort of thing."

"Okay. How about while I'm getting ice, I put some in a glass for you? With the drink of your choice, of course."

He nodded, not releasing her hand. His thumb circled her palm slowly, making her forget all about the burn. "How about, instead of that, I make us a couple of martinis, and you take it easy?" He scanned the kitchen and her handiwork. "I can see you've had quite a day. Everything looks and smells terrific."

"I hope you like chicken."

"My favorite."

"Carrots, too. Baked potatoes, salad. And a surprise for dessert."

His eyes widened fetchingly, and if she'd felt a smidgen more comfortable, she'd have leaned over and given him a big old kiss.

"So go get out of that necktie and wash up. It's all ready in, like, two minutes."

"Martinis first, then washing up."

"Uh-oh. Sounds like you had a day."

He went to the wet bar and picked up the bottle of gin. As he worked on the martinis, he told her about the couple who were having so much trouble conceiving. The story left her unsettled. She felt bad for the poor couple and nervous about her own risk, but there was something absolutely wonderful about listening to Mitchell's day, watching him as he fixed the drinks. She felt as if they'd been together always and had grown accustomed to each other in every way that mattered.

She'd never been this at ease with Tony. Not even after ten months of marriage. He'd hated her doing the cooking, insisting they either go out or have a cook in for the evening meal. At first it had been flattering. In the end, she realized his insistence had nothing to do with her. An evening without being photographed was an evening Tony was miserable. Which, in turn, meant she was miserable.

Mitch handed her a drink, his brow furrowed. "Her condition is very rare, Darcy. In fact, it's very rare for a woman to have any kind of inherent condition that prevents her from conceiving. It's what the female body is designed to do. So don't borrow trouble. You're probably as fertile as the old woman in the shoe.''

She smiled, touched by his concern. Amused at his analogy. There was no need to tell him her dismay was more about the past than the future. She lifted her glass. "To friendship."

"To friendship," he repeated. He sipped the cold drink, but his gaze never left her face. Particularly her eyes. He stared at her with an intensity that was a little daunting.

Mitch had such incredible focus. Ever since she'd known him, she'd been awed by his ability to concentrate so hard that the rest of the world disappeared for him. Nothing penetrated when he got like that.

He'd used that magic on her only twice. Once just before she'd left town. They'd been at the park having a deep, heartfelt discussion about their dreams. He'd listened to her like no other person in the world. Completely. Without any distraction. It had disconcerted her then, and it did now. He had narrowed the universe, blocking out everything but her. What was he seeing? What was he thinking? My God, what would it be like to be the object of that focus in bed?

It was too intense. She had to move, and the oven was the logical place to run. "Dinner's almost ready. You'd better go wash up."

"Right," he said, his voice softer than normal, as if he were waking up from a daydream. He left his drink on the wet bar and headed toward the stairs. She sighed once he was out of sight.

Something big was brewing tonight. She wasn't entirely sure what. The attraction she felt for him was stronger than ever. And unless her radar had gone completely wacky, it was mutual. The pull to touch him had an urgent quality, revving her heart, tightening her tummy. The need to be near him was so strong, his leaving the room left an ache inside her.

She got busy with the meal, needing to keep her hands and her thoughts occupied. She carved the chicken just the way Martha Stewart had taught her, and put the meat on a platter decorated with parsley and orange twists. The carrots went into a white ceramic bowl, and she sprinkled orange zest on top. She got the salad ready, and as she was pulling the baked potatoes from the oven, Mitch came back, his tie off, his white shirt open at the neck, sleeves rolled up to reveal muscled arms.

She fumbled the potatoes, dropping one on the open oven door. Luckily, it didn't fall out of its tinfoil packet.

"What can I do to help?" Mitch asked.

"Sit. It's all ready."

He grabbed his drink then sat at the table. "It's beautiful, Darcy."

"Aw, shucks."

"It is! I had no idea you knew how to cook like this."

"I took a class. Actually, several classes. Masochism, really. I couldn't eat ninety percent of what I cooked. The camera is a cruel, cruel thing."

"Then why put yourself through that?"

"Because I loved it. I think, if things had been different, I might have become a chef."

"I thought you wanted to be a science teacher or a doctor."

"Those, too."

"So what happened?"

She didn't answer right away. Instead, she brought the food to the table and pulled a nice bottle of white Zinfandel from the fridge. Once they were both set with dinner and she'd tasted the chicken to make sure it was just right, she turned to him. Ever since he'd left this morning, she'd been troubled by his strange comment. She had to find out what he meant. "Did you by any chance get a letter from me about two days before I left?"

He shook his head. "No."

Her chest tightened, and suddenly she wasn't hungry anymore. "Oh, God."

"What?"

"My mother. It had to have been her. Maybe she was afraid I wouldn't go."

"Darcy, what are you saying?"

"I wrote to you, Mitch. The letter explained that my father had run off with all our money, and that I'd been offered a contract with the Ford agency in New York and that I didn't want to go. I didn't want to leave school and I didn't want to be a model. But mostly, I didn't want to...well, you know."

He paled and put his fork down. She thought he was going to say something, but he didn't. He just stared at her, then at his plate. The silence ticked on, and in those quiet moments the enormity of what her mother had done seeped in. Everything had hinged on that letter. Everything she'd felt about Mitch, about herself and about men.

"I thought..."

"That I'd just left?"

He nodded. "I came to your house. She said you'd always wanted to be a model, and this was your chance. She said you couldn't wait to leave."

"And you believed her?"

His head turned slightly to the right. "She was your mother."

"You say that like it precludes her from doing something horrible."

"It never occurred to me. I figured I hadn't really known you. That I was just deluding myself that we had something between us."

Darcy sipped a little wine as she tried to keep calm. "You weren't deluding yourself. And it never occurred to you that someone's mother could be so deceitful. That's because you come from a healthy home. Megan would never do anything to hurt you."

"No, she wouldn't. I mean, we have our issues, but—"

"But your happiness means more to her than her own. I know that. I watched that all those years when I practically lived at your house. I didn't believe it at first. I thought it was an act for company. No family could be so happy, outside of *Leave It To Beaver* or something. But then…"

"We weren't that perfect."

"Compared to my life, you were."

His gaze settled on hers, and the look he gave her was more troubling than his confession. It was as if he were looking at a stranger. In a way, she supposed she was. "I'd convinced myself that I hadn't paid attention. That you had been my friend because… That you liked studying and I was the only other kid in the school who liked it as much."

"I did like studying, but that was hardly the reason I was your friend, Mitch. You knew me better than any other person in the world."

"I did?"

She nodded. Stared at her beautiful dinner growing cold. "I asked you to meet me in the park. I just knew that together we could come up with a plan to keep me in Austin. I waited for hours. I didn't go home until the sunrise."

His hand squeezed his glass so tightly she thought it would shatter. "You must have hated me," he said, his voice unrecognizably soft and tight.

"I did. But not for long. I realized you had your own life to live. That even if you had come to the park, there wasn't anything you could have done."

"I could have tried. My mother would have helped."

"Maybe. But maybe not. The important thing now is that we know the truth."

"Your whole life was taken from you."

"No, it wasn't. I've had an extraordinary life. Not at all what I'd have planned for myself, but hey." She shrugged. "I've met fascinating people. I've traveled all over the world. I've made a ton of money, and I don't have to worry for the rest of my life. It might not have been teaching science, but it had its advantages."

Mitch's frown deepened. She'd expected him to laugh. But maybe it was all too new to treat lightly. Before she could ask, he rose abruptly, knocking over his glass as he did. The wine spread across the table-cloth, but he didn't give it a second look. He crossed the room to the kitchen sink, turning so his back was to her.

She wanted to go to him, but his posture wasn't welcoming. In fact, it was just the opposite. If she didn't know better, she'd swear he was angry with her.

When he didn't move for an unbearably long time, she screwed up her courage. "Mitch?"

He whirled so suddenly it made her jump. "I'm sorry," he said, his gaze steady, confirming her suspicions about how angry he was.

"Why?"

"I should have realized."

"Mitch, you were seventeen. Hardly old enough to figure out my mother's Machiavellian plan."

The anger on his face shifted into a look of terrible pain. "I screwed up."

She rose and went over to him, but when she reached out her hand, she didn't touch him. "No, you didn't. It wasn't your fault."

"It never is."

"What?"

"Never mind." He stepped away from her, almost flinching at her nearness.

"Mitch, what's wrong? It was awful, I know that, but we weren't to blame. Neither of us."

He walked out of the kitchen, his shoulders hunched, his whole demeanor telling her he wanted to be left alone. They had both suffered a loss from this, not just him. So why had he run away? Could there be more to this story?

She drank some more wine, and realized she'd lost her appetite. Maybe later they'd sit down again, but for now, she'd put away the food. It gave her something to do, at least, while she wondered what demon had been stirred awake in Mitch.

When the table was clear and the candles extinguished, Darcy sat down, finally allowing herself to think. She remembered that night in the park, waiting for Mitchell. Praying for him to come. That was the night she realized there would be no Prince Charming, no knight on a white stallion to rescue her. If there was any rescuing to be done, she'd have to do it for herself. And that was exactly what she'd done.

But along with steely determination, that night had hammered home some other truths. That dreams were for children. That she couldn't count on anyone, not even her parents. That life was unfair, so she'd better make the best of the hand she'd been dealt.

Even though she hadn't ever felt pretty, she'd accepted that night that there was something about her face the modeling agency liked. Some trick of bone and shadow. Her prayers for a figure, for a bosom, for curves hadn't been answered, and yet it was her flaws they wanted. Too tall, too thin, too gangly…

If that's what they wanted, then that's what she'd give them. No more pigging out on ice cream or pizza. No more fast-food burgers and fries. If all she had was her face and figure, then she'd better take care of them.

She'd also realized, in a way so profound it chilled her heart, that her worth wasn't in her personality or her brains or her wit. Getting good grades meant nothing. All the things she'd felt too superior to care about—makeup, hairdos, clothes, shoes—were the very things her life would be centered around.

The irony was not lost on her. She'd just read Sartre's *No Exit,* and after that long night, when the sun had peeked above the horizon and she was still alone, she realized she had walked into her own personal hell. That she had no choice. That Mitch wasn't going to save her, even though she'd prayed harder than she'd ever prayed before. That she'd survived an earthquake of epic proportions, and the very ground beneath her feet had been shaken into dust. She wasn't going to be Darcy Taylor. Who she would become was a mystery.

Would he have been strong enough to keep her world intact? No. Not at seventeen. Not when her mother had been so determined. Mitch couldn't have saved her even if he had read the letter. He'd have met her in the park, and they would have said a tearful farewell. Perhaps her mother had been kind after all.

"Darcy?"

She whirled toward the doorway. Mitch seemed to have pulled himself together. His face was calm, and his eyes had lost their wildness. But something was still off.

"I'm sorry," he said as he joined her at the table. "I didn't mean to leave like that."

"It's all right. I've had all day to get comfortable with the idea."

"It's unsettling, all right." He picked up his wineglass, which she'd refilled—the only thing from dinner still left on the table. "I don't even know what to make of it. I'm glad you told me. But, damn it, I feel like I've stepped on a land mine."

"Why?"

He blinked at her question. She didn't back off. She

needed to know what he was feeling. What this meant to him.

He sipped his drink. Put the glass on the table. Cleared his throat. "I was in love with you," he said, the words as soft as a fading memory. "It broke my heart that you could leave me like that." His gaze settled on hers. "I would have done things differently."

"What?"

He gave her a sardonic smile. "Everything."

She touched his hand and sucked in a large breath at the contact. A jolt of awareness shot through her, and it wasn't just physical. The connection between them was stronger than that. Strong enough to travel through time. "You couldn't have saved me," she whispered.

"No?"

She shook her head sadly. "My mother wouldn't have let you."

"My family..."

"Couldn't have done a thing."

He squeezed her hand. "I could have come after you."

"And then what?"

He sighed. "I don't know."

"We had to go on our own roads, Mitch. No matter what the cause. I think it's important to see that the lie didn't kill either of us. It was horrible, but there's no use regretting what happened. And good things did happen. You went to medical school. I made oodles of money. You..." She leaned back a bit. "You met your wife."

His face changed. The melancholy in his eyes made her heart slow with sorrow.

"What's wrong?"

"Nothing."

"Mitch, please."

He mustered a smile. "It's nothing. Water under the bridge."

She nodded, unwilling to pry. But clearly his marriage wasn't a welcome topic. She wished she understood why.

"Why don't we finish that terrific dinner, huh?" He stood up, distancing himself from her. "Is it all back in the fridge?"

"Yeah."

He got busy bringing everything to the table, microwaving their plates, filling the wineglasses. Chatting about the food, the weather, nothing.

She knew so much about him. And she knew so little.

CHAPTER THIRTEEN

MITCH WASN'T SURE what to say. His mind still reeled from the repercussions of Darcy's announcement. She'd wanted him to save her. He hadn't. The recurring theme in his life.

Looking back, he could see all the signs that Darcy hadn't wanted to go. Why hadn't he seen them then? Was he stupid? Or had he just been so consumed with himself and his hormones that he couldn't see past his own nose?

What alarmed him almost as much as his self-recrimination was Darcy's reaction. She didn't seem very upset. But then, why would she be? Look at the life she ended up with. It would have been terrible if he'd stepped in to save her. He would have robbed her of her fame, her money, her adventures.

So now what? Her appetite seemed healthy enough. Not like his. He had to force himself to take a bite of the chicken, to chew, to swallow.

If he'd known about Darcy in college, would he have asked Angela on that first date? No. Probably not. Would he have accepted her love, even though he knew he could never return it in kind?

As sweet as Angela was, she had never occupied his heart fully, and she'd known it. All she'd asked of him was security and a child. Their child. But he hadn't been able to provide her with either one. Then she was gone.

So much like Darcy. Gone before he could do what was right. Damn it, he could have met her in the park. He could have gotten his mother to intercede. He could have...

He could have told her he loved her.

But he didn't, and then she was gone.

"Mitch, what is it?"

She put down her fork. Her brow creased as she stared at him, waiting. But what could he say?

Her hand came to rest on his, and a jolt went straight through him.

"You can tell me anything."

"Can I?"

She nodded. "Our lives seem to touch each other in odd places, don't you think? Like, maybe we're not done yet?"

"You really believe that?"

"Oh, yes. I don't think people come into our lives unless they're supposed to. It's all about lessons. Other people are our best teachers, especially the ones we're closest to."

"What's our lesson, Darcy?"

"I'm not sure yet. That's why we need to talk."

"You start."

Her smile was slow, reminiscent. "Some things never change."

"What do you mean?"

"Isn't that how we always began our discussions? I'd want to talk about something, and you'd tell me to start."

He nodded. "I suppose so. It worked, right?"

"That it did. Okay. Only it's hard to know where to begin this time."

"How about the day you left?"

She finished off her glass of wine and pushed her dinner plate away, leaving almost half her meal. "My mother sprang it on me two days before I got on the plane. I came home from the library, and my clothes were already packed."

"You didn't call me."

"She wouldn't let me."

"What?"

"She told me it would only make things more difficult. That the best way to handle this was just to leave. That I'd be so caught up in my new life I'd forget about you and everyone else."

"So you wrote the letter?"

"I thought I'd gotten away with it. I ended up asking Mrs. Baskin if she would take it to you."

"Your neighbor? The one with the poodles?"

Darcy nodded. "She must have told my mother about it."

Mitch couldn't eat any more, either. "Let's go in the other room."

As she stood, he was struck by her grace. So tall, nearly six feet, and yet so feminine. When she reached for his plate, he stopped her. "This can wait."

They moved together into the living room, but before she sat, she picked up their old yearbook. Then she got onto the couch, curling her long legs beneath her. He sat next to her, although not too close. He couldn't afford to be distracted by touching her. Not yet. Not until he heard it all.

Her hand rubbed the embossed cover of the book and her expression turned wistful. "Did you go to the prom?"

"Me? Yeah."

"I wish…"

"You didn't miss much. It was loud. There were too many people, and Elizabeth Masters was a royal pain in the butt. Literally. She was voted queen."

"No." Darcy's face scrunched up in distaste. "Who was king?"

He turned away.

"You? *You* were king of the prom?"

"I have no idea how it happened. In fact, I couldn't wait to get the hell out of there."

"Who did you bring?"

He met her gaze again. "No one."

"Seriously?"

"I wasn't exactly Mr. Popularity, you know."

"But so many girls liked you. I'd have thought they'd be lined up in droves."

"Me?" He sat back in surprise, wondering how she'd come up with that bit of fantasy. "I doubt it."

She laughed, a sound as familiar to him as his own sigh. "Oh, Mitchell. You didn't have a clue, did you?"

"About?"

"God, every girl in school thought you were a babe. They all hated me because I was your friend. They also thought we were closer than we actually were, if you get my drift."

"Are you kidding? I don't remember anything like that. I think you're thinking of someone else."

"I'm not. You weren't very observant about those

things. I think that was some of the appeal. A woman can pick that up in a guy. Even at that age.''

"This isn't making any sense, but it hardly matters now, does it?''

"No, it doesn't. Except that of all the things I've missed, the hardest was the prom.''

"Really?''

"I had a dress all picked out. It was at Darlene's, that dress shop on Fourth Street. I'd saved all my baby-sitting money so I could get that dress. It was so grown-up.''

"I wish I could have seen you in it.''

"I wish we'd danced.''

He laughed. "No you don't. Trust me. I had two left feet.''

"Oh, come on. Tell me you didn't dance with Elizabeth?''

"I didn't. It caused something of a furor, believe me. But I wouldn't do it.''

"She must have been so ticked off.''

"She was. Until I convinced Keith Banks to take my place.''

"Smart.''

"I had my moments.''

She flipped open the book and turned the pages slowly, her gaze lingering on long-ago friends and teachers. He watched her face. The way the corners of her lip lifted slightly, the shadow of her lashes on her cheeks. The way her hair fell across her temple. Her beauty almost hurt. It had been tough to look at her back then, but now? When she'd grown into such a stunning creature? How had that kind of beauty changed her? It had to have. No one could be unaffected by something so extraordinary.

"Oh, God, look."

He glanced down, following her finger. She pointed to a picture of him standing with a group of pathetic-looking boys. "The science club."

"You look adorable."

"You're crazy."

"No, I'm not. You're as cute as a button."

He didn't see it. All he saw was an awkward-looking teenager with unruly hair, big glasses and big feet.

"Those books. I can't believe it. You've even got them in the picture!"

He looked more closely. It was his biology text. Right where it always was.

"I was so intimidated by that."

"What?"

"The way you always had your books with you. How you studied all the time."

He grinned. Then laughed.

"What?"

"I wasn't studying all the time."

"Huh?"

"That's not why I carried the books."

"Then why?"

"I was seventeen. Think about it."

Her gaze went to the picture, and a few seconds later she burst out laughing. "Oh, poor baby! That must have been so uncomfortable."

"That's one way of saying it."

"I had no idea."

"Thank God."

"Was it all the girls, or just me?" she asked, wiggling her eyebrows with silly suggestiveness. Only it wasn't so silly.

"It was always just you."

Her brows stilled in the up position. He could see she hadn't expected that.

"Darcy, didn't you know? Didn't you see?"

"Obviously not."

"I wasn't kidding before. I was crazy about you."

"You mean, crazy like in love crazy?"

He nodded. "Crazy like in love."

"Oh, my."

She closed the book, and her eyes. Leaned her head back on the sofa. For a long time, the only thing that moved was her chest as she breathed.

Finally she looked at him again. "I loved you, too."

He tried to say something, but his voice didn't work.

"I loved you for years. Even after—"

"After I didn't come rescue you?"

"Even after that."

"Why didn't you say anything?"

"For the same reason you didn't. I was shy, gawky, inept. I'd never liked anyone before, and I never was sure what you felt about me."

He shook his head. "Thank God we don't have to do that again. Go back, I mean."

"I know," she agreed. "Puberty sucked."

He laughed again. "Yes, indeed."

"Maybe we could go back for a day, hmm? Just a day?"

"What would you do?"

Her gaze grew quite serious. "I'd take you behind the gym by the bleachers. And I'd tell you the whole truth. That I loved you. That I dreamed of you and thought of you all the time. That I had a whole notebook filled with Mr. and Mrs. Mitchell Maitland written in it, in every conceivable form. And then..."

He leaned toward her, hardly believing what he was hearing. He'd dreamed of her, too. And she was never far from his thoughts. He hadn't had the notebook, but he'd done the equivalent, which was to keep her picture tucked away inside the pages of a contraband *Playboy* magazine. "And then?"

"I would have kissed you."

"Brazen."

She nodded. "Brazen and wicked and all the other things I was too timid to explore."

"You're not too timid now, are you?"

She shook her head, but before she stilled, he leaned over and kissed her. It was the purest sensation he'd ever known. As if they were those shy teenagers behind the gym, exploring each other for the first time.

Her hand went to his neck, and she pulled him tighter against her. His rib hit the yearbook, and he broke the kiss long enough to grab it and toss it on the floor. Then he took her in his arms, but not as a boy. He took her as the man he was now. With twenty years of passion coursing through his veins.

He stood, lifting her with him, holding tight to her arms, afraid to let go for fear she'd disappear. His mouth touched hers, and her response was instant and electric. She kissed him boldly, opening her mouth to him, exploring in return.

Her body rubbed against him, causing an immediate urgent reaction. No textbooks tonight. No hiding his feelings or his response to her.

He rubbed her back, letting her know just what she did to him. What she'd always done.

Her moan told him a great deal. Her hand running down his back told him more.

He eased out of the kiss, capturing her gaze. "Darcy…"

"Yes."

"I want you."

She nodded. "Oh, God, yes."

"Are you sure?"

"It's taken so long to get here," she said. "You're not getting rid of me so easily."

He kissed her again, the last shred of reserve fading with the taste of her on his lips, on his tongue. The woman he'd dreamed about from his earliest awareness of the difference between boys and girls was his. And she wanted him in return. The woman in the magazines had come to life.

It was her turn to ease away. She took his hand in hers and led him toward the staircase. Her pace quickened with each step, so that by the time they'd hit the stairs, they were practically running.

But once inside his bedroom, she stopped stock-still.

"What's wrong."

"This isn't your bedroom."

"Pardon?"

She laughed, but it sounded self-conscious. "I know it's ridiculous, but I always pictured your old bedroom. That plaid bedspread. The picture of Einstein on the wall.''

''He's in the kitchen now.''

''I saw.''

''You know, Darcy, that bed was a twin.''

''Was it? I didn't think of that.''

''And—'' he took her hand and pulled her inside the master suite ''—my sisters were right next door. They would've heard everything.''

''Hmm. I never realized the logistics would be so tricky.''

''Ah, but things change.''

''They do?''

He nodded. ''No one can hear us tonight.''

''And the bed is certainly large enough.''

''You see? It's all working out just fine.''

Her eyes caught his once more. ''Hey, Maitland.''

''What, Taylor?''

She grabbed him by the belt and pulled him close. After a light, seductive kiss, she smiled. ''My dreams always ended before the good stuff.''

''Then we'll have to use my dreams, won't we?''

Her laugh was mischievous, and where her hand had gone was downright wicked.

CHAPTER FOURTEEN

DARCY FELT his hardness beneath her hand, and a thrill of excitement ran through her from top to toe. They were going to make love. Finally, the big question was going to be answered. She'd always imagined they would be spectacular in bed. Perhaps she had set herself up for disappointment, but she didn't think so. Not with the way she felt when he kissed her.

Mitch moaned as she touched him, and his mouth became more insistent and intimate. She gave as good as she got, abandoning herself to the fantasy come true. She wouldn't think about her old doubts, not tonight. Not with him.

Instead, she pressed herself against his body, and when he reached down to pull up her shirt, she offered no resistance. He stepped back, pulling her top over her head, leaving her in her bra.

His gaze went to her breasts. She reached back, unhooking the silky material. But she didn't drop the garment. She held it up with one hand and lowered the straps with the other in a sort of slow striptease. She heard his intake of breath a second before she released the bra, letting it fall to the floor.

He devoured her with his gaze. But it wasn't the same as it had been with Tony or either of the other two men she'd been with. Mitch was looking at *her*. Not the model, not the celebrity. This wasn't a wet-dream fantasy that had nothing to do with her heart or her soul. This was Mitch, the boy she'd loved. The man she admired. Her friend, and now her lover.

His hands went to his shirt, but she stepped over to him, pushed his fingers away and did the job herself. He smiled at her, his hands touching her naked back, rubbing her skin in slow circles as she undid button after button, finally pulling his shirt out of his trousers.

A moment later, they were both bare on top. He pulled her close so her chest was pressed against his. Along with the distinct eroticism, there came an equally distinct calm. How she could feel both things at once was a mystery too big for her. All she knew was that even though she'd never been here before, she was home. She closed her eyes and rested her head on his shoulder as he continued to massage her back.

"Darcy," he whispered. "Are you all right?"

"Oh, much more than that."

"I'm glad."

She smiled, then kissed his shoulder. After that, she moved her head so she could nibble his neck. He moaned again, and she became aware that he was about to break his zipper if they didn't do something soon.

Reaching down to his belt, she pulled the leather through the loop, and it occurred to her just then that this might be the answer to a different prayer. What if Mitch, tonight, became the father of her child? What if they didn't use protection at all, and…

She put the brakes on her fevered thoughts. There was no way she could ask him to do anything of the sort. Nor would she trick him into it. Although the idea of Mitch fathering her child was incredibly wonderful, tonight wasn't the night to bring it up. The relationship was still too new, too amorphous.

There was no doubt in her mind that she wanted him this way. But she wasn't sure what would happen next. There were too many unanswered questions to do something as reckless as getting pregnant with Mitch tonight.

"What's wrong?"

She realized her hands had stopped before completing her task. She looked at him. "Nothing. Except that I'm nervous."

His brows came down immediately. "We can stop right here. Right now."

"No. That's not what I'm nervous about."

"What, then?"

"It's silly."

"Tell me. It's okay."

She took in a deep breath, then let it out slowly, blowing the air onto the smattering of dark hair on his chest. "I haven't done this very often."

"No?"

"Don't sound so shocked. Just because I've been around the block doesn't mean I've slept in all the beds along the way."

His laughter made his body vibrate against her, and she finished undoing his belt.

"So you're nervous that I won't have a good time?"

"Sort of," she said.

His finger went to her chin, and he lifted her gaze to meet his. "There's nothing to worry about."

"Ah, you're just saying that."

He shook his head. "Oh, no. Just touching you makes me ache inside. Feeling you next to me is the best thing that's happened to me in years."

"You mean it?"

He sighed, shaking his head in mock disapproval. "Don't you get it?"

"Hmm?"

"I'm crazy about you."

The words made her tremble. She wanted them to be true. Maybe magic did happen. Maybe they were destined to be together, and they could spend the rest of their lives learning about each other.

When he kissed her this time, the slow seduction was over. His hungry lips stole her breath, and his right hand moved to cup her breast. They moaned together, and a second later, he attacked his zipper and she took off her pants and undies in record time.

Naked, excited, they stared at each other for a long moment. His gaze moved down her body with a look of reverence she'd never seen before. He didn't seem to care that her thighs were heavier than *Vogue* liked them, or that her waist was an inch and a half thicker than Claudia's. He didn't see any of the flaws the camera focused on, the hundred little items the airbrush erased before her image made the magazine.

She let herself enjoy the sight of him. His broad shoulders, the dark hair covering the well-defined muscles of his chest. The way that dark hair tapered to a slim line leading her eyes to his erection. "Oh, my," she whispered as she looked at him. It took her several seconds to move her gaze down his legs, and while she appreciated that his legs were top notch, she really needed to look up again.

He didn't give her much time, though. Instead, he took her hand and led her toward the bed. He tossed the comforter back, lifted all six feet of her and laid her on the mattress. She held out her hand, and he took it, joining her in his bed.

As soon as he was prone, he shifted toward her and pulled her into his embrace. Kisses once more. Long, slow, hot kisses that stole her reason. She kissed him back in a way that was totally unique. With hunger, with joy, his taste, his scent filling her with fire.

He pulled back, adjusting himself so she fit snugly in the curve of his arms. His hand traveled down her chest and stopped at her breasts. He caressed her gently, and her nipples, already thickening, became hard nubs.

With the hands of a surgeon—no, the hands of a lover—he stroked her, moving his palms across the sensitive buds until she thought she would go mad with the overwhelming sensations. Impatient, sensitized and ready for him, she moved her hand down his chest and his tight stomach until her fingers brushed the curly hair just above the junction of his thighs.

She touched him there for the first time. Felt his flesh and his heat. Felt the size of him, the astonishing softness of the skin encasing the rock-hard member.

He groaned as she encircled him and moved her hand up and down his length, and as she did so, he got even firmer, thicker.

His mouth found hers again, and his hand moved

from her breasts, skimming her waist and her belly until he hesitated at the small vee of hair. His pause spoke loudly. "Bathing suits," she whispered.

"Hmm?"

"I have to keep it trimmed like that for bathing suits."

His fingers inched down, past the small triangle to the smooth lips of her sex. She heard him take a sharp breath as he caressed her. "It's the softest thing I've ever felt."

"It is?"

He nodded. "But I bet I can find someplace even softer."

Before she had a chance to guess where, his index finger slid inside her. With unerring grace he found the most sensitive spot on her body and proceeded to very gently rub in tight circles.

The effect was electric and immediate. Her muscles stiffened, and from his yelp, so had her grip on him. She eased up, but he didn't. He kept at it, circling, just the perfect amount of pressure, and when her body needed more, he sensed it by magic.

"Darcy," he whispered. "I've thought of this, of you, for so long."

She nodded, wanting it all. Wanting every inch of him inside her. Wanting to know him completely, and for him to know her just as well. "Please," she said, her thought inarticulate, her voice small. Her need overpowering.

"Yes," he said, but his finger left her and he rocked away, leaving her. She heard a drawer open. The sound of tearing told her what he was doing, and for a crazy moment she thought about stopping him.

She didn't want him to wear the condom. Not just because she wanted a child, but because she didn't want to miss a single sensation.

But she kept silent as he rolled back, as he kissed her, as he straddled her body.

She spread her legs with no self-consciousness at all. Closed her eyes, waiting for the moment of their joining, but it didn't happen.

Instead, he broke his kiss and slipped down the bed, hesitating to take her right nipple into his mouth, then her left. He didn't linger there long. His tongue traced a path down her tummy to the small vee.

And then he kissed her on her nether lips. Gently. He lifted his mouth, blew a soft, hot stream of air on the spot he'd kissed, then his mouth came down again, this time so he could slip inside her.

She started shaking immediately. Her hands had to do something when she discovered he was even more talented with his tongue than his fingers. She grabbed his hair, trying not to hurt him. Trying to hang on for dear life.

He moaned as if he was in ecstasy, too, which confused her. No man had ever... Not like this. Not with such obvious pleasure. His finger slipped inside her once more, not dislodging his mouth but moving inside her with a whole new rhythm.

As she pulsed with hot need, he increased the tempo of his tongue and his lips and then his finger, strong, insistent, all the way in, mimicking the act she wanted so badly she was about to scream. Just as it became unbearable, when every muscle was at the snapping point, he slipped out of her, moved up her body and thrust into her with his thick heat.

She wasn't sure what the sound was that came out of her. A scream, a sigh, a prayer. But it was all she could do when her mind and her spirit were entwined with Mitchell's, when she was nothing but sensation and pleasure.

And he kept on, fitting inside her perfectly, building the pressure, sending them straight toward climax with the relentlessness of the tide.

She crested first to that indescribable moment when time stops, when the gratification is so intense it transports the very soul. A second later, he came with a howl of pure animal satisfaction, trembling inside her, so deep, so perfect, it was if she had been designed for this moment.

It was bliss. It was so much better than her dreams, than her imagination could have predicted. She'd had no idea it could be like this. None.

He groaned, coming out of the climax, and she squeezed her muscles to help him along. His gasps told her he liked it. His kiss told her he liked her.

But, as with all things, the moment came to an end. He moved to her side, slipping out of her. Cuddling, their bodies touching from shoulder to toe.

"Oh, my sweet heaven," she whispered.

"Uh-huh."

"I mean…"

"I know."

"It's never—"

"Really?"

"Really."

He smiled at her. "It's never—for me, either."

"Really?"

He nodded.

"Well, how do you like that?"

He chuckled softly. "I like it a lot, Taylor. One hell of a lot."

SARA PICKED UP the phone, then put it down again. It was torture not understanding what was going on and worse torture realizing that if she asked for help, it might lead to her downfall.

Someone had tried to kill her. Of that, she felt positive. The Lexus had missed her by a hair, and if she hadn't jumped out of the way...

Her grave would have been marked Sara. No last name. Or perhaps they'd have used the anonymous Doe. But whatever name they used, it wouldn't be hers.

Who would come to the funeral? The folks at work, bless them. But they were only friends to this woman with the made-up name, with the made-up life. They would have no stories, no history to share with each other.

This couldn't go on. Not knowing was going to make her insane. And now she knew the feelings she'd been having all week were legitimate. Someone had been watching her.

But why? What on earth could she have done that was so bad someone wanted her dead?

She got up from her bed and paced across the room. She touched her hairbrush. The little bottle of inexpensive perfume she'd bought two weeks ago. Nothing felt right or looked right.

Did she have a signature fragrance? A special way of doing her hair, her makeup?

She closed her eyes, trying to remember. Anything. *Anything*.

That name. Connor.

Was he someone from her past? A husband? A son? The man behind the wheel of the Lexus? If only she'd gotten the license plate number. Maybe someone could have helped.

And then it occurred to her. Beth's fiancé. What was his name? So good-looking. Nice, too. Maybe he would help her. Maybe he could somehow find out the truth. A truth that might save her…or condemn her.

God help her, she was terrified. All she wanted was peace. In her heart, in her soul and in her mind. Peace, tranquillity, safety. But until she figured out who she was and who was trying to kill her, there would be no peace.

She went to the phone and picked it up again. She dialed the main switchboard at Maitland, a number she knew by heart since so many of the doctors and nurses ate at Austin Eats. She listened to the ring, once, twice, and then a voice.

Sara put the phone down, severing the connection. Her hand trembled, and her heart hammered in her chest. And then the tears came.

She fell on the bed and buried her face in her pillow to muffle her sobs.

CHAPTER FIFTEEN

MITCH STARED at the little light beneath the bathroom door. She'd be coming out any second now.

In all his years, he'd never experienced anything close to making love with Darcy. Of course, it had everything to do with fulfilling his fantasies—the longest-running fantasies in history, he supposed. But when he compared the experience to other, less stellar moments of wish fulfillment, he realized that each of those had left him somewhat dissatisfied. The dream had far outdone the reality.

Not this time.

He'd never felt anything as good as her. As soft. As perfect. He'd never wanted anyone more. Since the first kiss he'd felt an overwhelming need to touch her, to make certain she was real, and really here.

Not to mention the sex.

He was no Lothario, but he wasn't a hermit, either. Yet even his first time paled in comparison. Darcy had been—

The door opened. She walked out, backlit in a halo of golden light. Her hair, thick, tousled, framed the most beautiful face in the world. The slim, long body curved deliciously at the waist, flared slightly at the hips. He found it a little hard to breathe.

When she got to the bed, her smile made her real

again. The smile that hadn't changed in all these years. Of course, he knew that wasn't true, but the way she held her mouth, the way she quirked her lips... Her smile was what he'd looked at first in all the pictures over the years. Sometimes he'd barely recognized her with different hair color and wild makeup. But the smile had given her away every time.

"What's that grin for?"

He hadn't realized he'd been smiling, too. "Oh, I don't know."

She scooted close, fitting against him perfectly, her head resting on his shoulder, her arm across his chest. Then he felt her leg cross him, and he knew that he'd have to show inordinate self-control not to make love to her again in the next five seconds.

"It's earlier than I thought," she said, her warm breath hitting him on the neck, giving him gooseflesh.

"I know. Hard to believe it's not even eleven." He shifted his gaze so he could see her. "Did you have a late-night assignation or something?"

"Nope. I'm just where I want to be."

He touched her arm, rubbing the smooth skin lightly. "You're just where I want you to be, too."

She kissed his neck. Then sighed.

"I meant to ask you earlier. Charlotte tells me you're going to announce your retirement."

"Yep. The press conference is set for tomorrow."

"Are you okay with everything?"

"No, but I'll get over it. It's not as if I have a great deal of choice."

"Ouch."

"I don't mean that. It was a pipe dream that the

press wouldn't have found out I was here. I meant that being a public figure makes living a normal life virtually impossible.''

"I'd always thought of it as glamorous.''

She laughed. "I'd say about one percent of my life is glamorous. The rest has been very tiring.''

"I'm sorry. I'd hoped it had turned out well for you.''

"It has. I'm not complaining, honestly. No one knows better than I that I got the brass ring. At least, in some ways.''

"But now you've changed carousels.''

"Exactly. The old one isn't going to let go so easily.''

"It's going to be fine,'' he said. "I'm not even sure how I know that, but I do.''

"Thanks for the vote of confidence. I'll expect to hear that again tomorrow night, after the press conference.''

"Do you want me to go? I'm sure I can juggle my patients.''

"No, no. You don't have to. Your family has already been in the press too much lately. Hank will take care of me. He always does.''

Mitch closed his eyes for a moment as he reveled in the feel of her. "I'm still sorry. I wish I'd handled things differently.''

"Please, Mitch. It's not your fault.''

"You're a very beautiful liar.''

"Ha.''

"I don't know,'' he said, after giving her arm a gentle squeeze. "I suppose having you here flustered me. I've never been indiscreet before, and we've got plenty of famous clients.''

''You gonna beat yourself up with this for long? If you are, I'm going to the kitchen.''

''No. No, I'm not. Are you hungry?''

''A little. But not enough to do anything about it.''

''I can go get you something.''

''No, you can't. You're not leaving this bed. Maybe never.''

He turned so he could see her fully, even though he hated to dislodge her arm. ''This is pretty unbelievable, isn't it?''

She nodded. ''I was so unsure.''

''About?''

''Coming back. Seeing you.''

''I'm glad you did.''

She lifted her head. ''Are you?''

''God, Darcy, yes. I can still hardly believe it. I mean, you, in my bed. In my life. It's like something out of a movie.''

Her head crooked a bit, then he heard her sigh as she lay against him once more.

''What?''

''Nothing.''

But it wasn't nothing. He felt her body stiffen. Not much, but enough for him to know he'd said something wrong. ''Hey, Taylor?''

''Yeah?

''Did I say something?''

''No.''

''You sure?''

''Will you do me a favor?''

''Anything.''

"Make love to me."

He moaned his answer as he turned to oblige.

MEGAN GENTLY PATTED Chase's tiny back, encouraging him to burp after his bottle. The little one was growing and changing before her very eyes.

Poor Janelle. It must be so hard on her not being able to take the baby home. But the county was excruciatingly slow getting the birth records, and Megan's pleas to have Social Services alter their procedure had fallen on deaf ears.

She took a deep breath, luxuriating in the baby's distinct, soothing fragrance. As bad as she felt for Janelle and Connor, she had to confess that she would be heartsick to see Chase go. He delighted her in every way. His soft skin, his tiny hands and feet. His smile when he heard her voice. If only she could keep him. Watch him grow, just as she'd watched her own children. It was a selfish wish, she knew that. But she couldn't help it. She'd come to love Chase. Love him with all her heart.

Glancing at the clock, she realized that she wouldn't be going back to bed, even though she was tired. It was six-thirty, and there was so much to do with the gala so soon. Her to-do list was a joke. But she'd get it done. Her children would help, thank goodness. They were such good kids.

A very large belch broke the still morning. "My, my, that was a mighty roar," she said as she rocked him back and forth on the chair William had bought her when their first baby was born.

Her nostalgia was short-lived. Thoughts of the gala intruded, and with them came a sense of unease that had been lurking in the back of her mind for quite some time. Something told her it wasn't the anniversary party that had her troubled, though.

The problem was, she didn't know what was wrong. She'd come to rely on her intuition more and more as the years went by. And a warning bell was going off. But why?

Maybe it was all the recent trouble. Or maybe it *was* the gala, and she had forgotten something big. Or maybe it was her meeting yesterday with Harrison Smith. This time, she'd seen him alone, leaving Mitch out of the picture. Mr. Smith had been cordial and astute, and his questions, like those during the first meeting, were of a strange, almost intrusive nature. Not that he'd been inappropriate, but still…

There was something about the man.

No use worrying about it. She'd find out what was going on eventually. Trouble was an old friend. One she'd learned not to panic about. When calm heads prevailed, answers came.

Chase burped again, a small one this time, and she looked at his beautiful face. He was inches from sleep, his little eyelids opening and shutting until finally they didn't open again.

Such a sweet, innocent child. She wished she had the power to save him from trouble, but she didn't. She couldn't protect him. She'd never been able to protect her own children. Life would have its way. Trouble happened. And with each new problem came growth. And strength. And, when she was very lucky, a new closeness to those she loved.

"I'll always be here for you, my precious," she whispered. "No matter what."

DARCY STOPPED EATING when the weather person came on television. It was going to be a nice day. Perfect, in fact. Not too humid, not too hot. That was good. The press were always crankier when the weather was miserable.

She took another bite of toast as her gaze went to the man sitting across from her. Mitchell, cleaned up and fresh from the shower—their shower—looked good enough to eat. His dark hair was slightly damp, his face smoothly shaven, and she detected a twinkle in his eyes that had been put there early this morning.

They'd made love before the alarm had gone off. It had been slow and sweet, not at all like last night's urgent mating. This morning had been perhaps less extravagant, certainly less athletic, but to her, it had been the best time of all.

They'd made love like any couple would in the morning. Any couple who cared about each other. Who wanted to be close. Who understood each other. She felt as if Mitchell had always been there for her, and in a way, she supposed he had.

Except…

Except for one comment last night. One little thing. She was blowing it out of proportion, that's all. He hadn't meant anything by it. Surely not the way she'd heard it.

Mitchell's disbelief that she was in his life had nothing to do with modeling or fame. Of course it didn't. He'd been referring to their past together, that's all.

She should forget about it. Wasn't it because she knew him so well that she'd come back? She could have gone anywhere, but Mitch was where she felt safest. Nothing had changed about that. Except that after last night, she knew her decision had been the right one.

He wasn't enamored of her public image. He'd known her too long for that. With him, she was just Taylor. Not an icon, not a sex object—

Wait. She wanted to be a sex object to him. Just not the kind she'd been to so many men in the last few years. Including her husband.

Not once, in all her adult life, had she believed that the man in her bed was there because of who she was on the inside. Until now. Until Mitch.

"What's that look for?"

"Do I have a look?"

"Uh-huh. A pretty damn happy one."

"Must be the coffee," she said.

"You haven't had any yet."

"Oh, yeah."

He got up and came around behind her. His hands went to her shoulders, and then he kissed her cheek. It was a totally novel sensation, but utterly comfortable, like an old, favorite sweater. She breathed deeply, relishing his scent. No aftershave or cologne. Just clean and male. An intoxicating combination, one designed to make her forget about the rest of her day, the rest of his day, and beg him to stay home.

"I've got to go," he said, popping her bubble.

She stood to face him, and his thumb went to the corner of her mouth. She must have had a crumb, but now it was gone. "Hey, Maitland?"

"Yeah, Taylor?"

"After the press conference, I won't need to stay here any longer. I'll be able to go home."

The look he gave her was the exact response she'd hoped for. Disappointment. He didn't want her to go. She didn't want to go. But...

"You're welcome here."

"Am I?"

He kissed her. Hard. His hands pressing her to him. The warmth of his lips traveling deep inside to a place that had been cold for so long.

And when he pulled back, breaking the kiss, the warmth was still in his eyes.

"Walk out with me?" he asked.

She nodded. He led her to the garage, and after he pushed the door opener, he took her to the driver's side of his car. He stopped and leaned close for another kiss. The moment his lips touched hers, a flash of light hit her square in the face. Darcy leaped back, the adrenaline in her body spiking in the basic urge to fight or flee.

Mitchell spun around, and they saw the reporter at the same second. The bastard must have been camping there all night. He was young, nineteen or so, and he kept snapping picture after picture even as he backed away.

When Mitch went after him, she felt a flash of panic. If he got hurt...

"Who are you, you son of a bitch?" Mitch demanded, striding toward him.

"The press," the boy said, quickening his pace.

"This is private property. How did you get in here?"

"Doesn't matter. She's not private property."

"That's where you're wrong, sonny." Mitch marched after him relentlessly, and the boy turned to look behind him, but a truck, the *Tattle Today* truck, blocked him. He made a dart to the right, but Mitch was too fast for him. He grabbed the kid's arm and pushed him against the truck.

"When she's with me," Mitch said, his voice ominous, his stance more so, "she's private. And you're trespassing. I'm going to call the police chief, who happens to be a close friend, and oh, what the hell, I'll just beat the crap out of you myself."

"No!" Darcy called frantically. She made it to Mitch's side in an instant. "He's not worth it."

"I agree," a cool feminine voice replied. "But it would look marvelous on the six o'clock edition."

Chelsea Markum stepped out of the van, looking as if she'd just come from makeup. She smiled at Mitch, then at Darcy. For a split second, Darcy thought she saw something flicker in her eyes. Sympathy? Compassion?

No. Impossible. The woman had camped out here, hoping to get something on Mitch. On her. She was a vulture, and like all vultures, she was dangerous all the time.

"What do you want?" Mitch asked her.

"Information."

Darcy moved beside him and pulled him back a little, since he was still menacing the photographer. "There's a press conference today at three. You'll get what you want then."

Chelsea shook her head. "Not good enough. I want something exclusive."

"Tough," Mitch said. "Get out before I call the police."

"Are you the father?" Chelsea asked him, as if he hadn't just threatened her.

"The father of what?"

"Darcy's baby?"

"What?"

"You yourself said she was a patient. And you don't exactly run a foot hospital, now, do you?"

"I don't believe this. Lady, you are way out of bounds."

"Am I?"

"Haven't you learned anything in the last few months? You've been wrong about my family so many times it's getting to be a joke. Don't you get tired of it? Being wrong?"

"No. It all comes with the territory. I might be wrong about this, too. But I'm not giving up until I know for sure."

"Then be sure," Darcy said. "I'm not pregnant."

Chelsea's gaze shifted toward her. "Are you trying to be?"

"That is *so* none of your business."

The reporter's laugh traveled down the empty street. "Everything is my business," she said. "Especially when the world's top-paid model comes home to my turf. And when that model has caused all sorts of problems for one of the largest makeup manufacturers in the world. And even more so when she's a patient at Maitland Maternity. Are you starting to see my position?"

"Yes," Darcy agreed. "It's easy to see your position. Just like it's easy to see why the shark attacks the helpless boy on the raft. But with people, there are consequences. There are supposed to be judgment calls. Maybe even respect for the rights of others.''

''You can't be that naive. You've been around too long for that.''

''I'm not. But I always hope. If I gave up hoping, why, then I'd probably be just like you.''

Chelsea's cheeks reddened, but her steely gaze never faltered. ''I'm not going to let it go.''

''You know, honey,'' Darcy said, ''I was pretty sure you were going to say that.''

''So why not make it easy on both of us, and tell me what you're really doing here.'' The woman's cool gaze moved to Mitchell. ''And what you're doing as a patient at Maitland Maternity.''

Darcy sighed. ''No. I'm not going to make anything easier on you. In fact, I'll make it as difficult as I can. I thought I saw some spark of humanity in your eyes, but I guess that was just a trick of the light.''

''Oh, please,'' Chelsea said. ''Spare me.''

''That's enough.'' Mitch moved between Darcy and the reporter. ''It's time for you to leave now. And I'm going to make sure the police are here tonight, checking for intruders.''

''It's all going to come out, you know,'' Chelsea said as she headed for the truck. ''There's no way you can keep this kind of thing a secret.''

Mitch turned toward Darcy. ''Are you going to be okay?''

She nodded, ignoring the sound of the truck behind them and the last flash of the photographer's bulb. ''I'll be fine.''

''I meant it about staying here.''

"Thanks. I'm not sure what's best yet. I need to talk to Hank. And to see what happens this afternoon."

"Where is the press conference?"

"At the Hyatt. But don't worry about it. It's going to be fine."

He leaned toward her but stopped himself before he touched her. Instead, he took her hand in his and squeezed it. "Hey, Taylor."

She smiled. "Hey, Maitland."

"I'll talk to you later."

She nodded, a strange lump forming in her throat. Disappointment. She'd thought, just for a second, that he was going to tell her... What? That he loved her? How could he?

Did she love him? No. It couldn't possibly be. Not this soon. Not this hard.

She loved what they'd done together. What they meant to each other. But she didn't love him. Not yet.

CHAPTER SIXTEEN

IT TOOK MITCH the whole ride to the clinic to calm down about Chelsea Markum. Even then, he hadn't made peace with the unbelievable intrusion, but he had come to see that the best way to handle such things was the way Darcy had. Take the high road. Ignore as much as possible. Don't let them get to you.

But damn it, he wanted to do something. By nature, he wasn't a passive man, although there weren't many people who understood that about him. His mother had always known his rash side. With her help, he'd learned how to curb his temper and to think things through. If it hadn't been for Megan, he'd never have gotten through medical school, and he certainly wouldn't have made it through Angela's illness.

But now that he thought about it, wasn't that the common thread between the important women in his life? All three of them were patient as saints, and all three of them knew how to get him to think before he acted.

He pulled into his parking place and turned off the ignition, but he didn't get out of his car immediately. His thoughts, while they should be squarely focused on the incredible night he'd had, were on Angela.

Poor Angela. Even when it had been the very best between them, it had never been like last night. He

wasn't denying a connection and a real affection between them, but with Angela, the relationship was
more cerebral. Until the end, of course. That had been
anything but cerebral.

The smell of the hospital room was still vivid in
his memory, not like the smell in the nursery or even
in the OR. Angela's room had smelled of defeat.

A life cut short. A promise unfulfilled. And not
even the legacy of a child to mark that she'd once
been on this earth. She'd had no family to speak of,
and the one aunt they'd found living in a double-wide
trailer in Henderson, Nevada, had died two months
after Angela.

And that was that. Nothing left. No stories about
the old-timers, no pictures to pass down, no one to
cherish the memory of a wonderfully nice woman
he'd had the good fortune to know.

God, he hadn't thought about her this much since
her death. He pushed open his car door and got out,
forcing himself to focus on his day.

But as he got into the elevator, he heard the soft
sound of weeping. He couldn't see who it was and
had no idea why the woman was crying. Except that
it had everything to do with having babies. Because
when a woman was denied that, she was denied a
major reason for her existence.

Of course there were women who didn't want children, and in his opinion there was nothing wrong with
that. In fact, better to face the responsibilities head-
on and make a decision that was best for all.

But the women who came to him hadn't made that
choice. Not voluntarily. They desperately wanted a

child, and they wanted it to be of their flesh and blood.

The elevator door closed with a whisper, and the crying stopped. He hoped they were tears of joy, although he didn't think so.

He got to the second floor, and the doors opened. A flash, just like the one this morning, hit him in the eyes. His fury rose, stronger than ever. What was the stupid son of a bitch trying to do? He'd never talk about Darcy.

It was hard to see, but Mitch headed straight for the guy with the camera. In fact, he surprised the jerk, grabbing his shirt with his right hand, flexing his left for a nice hook across the chin.

"Whoa, hold on there, Doc."

The voice wasn't the same as this morning. It didn't matter. One jaw was as good as the next.

"Hey, Doc Maitland, hold on! I'm sorry. I shouldn't have surprised you like that, but Ellie said she wanted me to take candid shots of all the docs for the gala."

"Ellie?" Mitch's left fist loosened. His right kept hold of the young man's shirt.

"Ellie, as in your sister." The photographer, who was finally coming into focus, looked to be about twenty and was not even close to the description of the guy in his front yard. "I'm Frank," he said, trying to hold out his hand to shake, but not succeeding very well. Not that it was his fault. Mitch had him up on his toes and was probably cutting off a good deal of his air supply.

Mitch let him go, and Frank stumbled. His pale

face got a little pink, and he rubbed the back of his neck while he stared at Mitch with accusatory eyes.

"I'm sorry. I thought you were someone else."

"I'd hate to be that poor dude."

"Yes, you would. And please tell Ellie that candid shots of clinic employees is perhaps not the wisest course of action."

Frank nodded, never blinking, never letting Mitch out of his sight until he had hit the back wall of the elevator. "Right away, Doc. Right away."

The elevator took him away. Mitch stood in the hall, focusing on his breathing, trying once more to calm himself. He'd had so much adrenaline pumping through him this morning he'd insult any cup of coffee he drank.

The life of a celebrity really was something awful. Worse than being a Maitland these past few months. No privacy. Unpleasant surprises at all hours. No, thank you.

DARCY'S HEART SANK as she turned the last corner. The crowd, despite the announcement about the press conference, was still thick. Reporters and photographers had staked out her street, and it was foolish to think she could get past them.

She kept on driving, circling toward Mitch's place.

Why had she been surprised? She knew the press better than most people, and the idea that they would all hear the information about her at once wouldn't please anyone. But damn, all she wanted was to go to her own home. To sit on her own couch. To open her own refrigerator.

But it wasn't all bad. She got to go back to Mitch's.

Of course, it would have been better if she'd gone back because she wanted to, not because she had to.

Hey, she did want to. Very, very badly. It was only that...

She pulled up to the private gate at his development and punched in Mitch's code. But she didn't go inside. Instead, she turned the car around and headed toward the center of town.

JANELLE WATCHED as Petey fixed himself a sandwich. He hummed, a tuneless, monotonous sound that grated on every one of her nerves. He didn't even know he was humming. But he was, and that told her a lot. Petey only hummed when he was up to something. She recognized all the signs. His few tiny brain cells had kicked into gear and given him a thought.

She'd tried, early on, to break him of the annoying habit, but then she'd let it go. It was useful to know when Petey got to thinking. Most of the time, it was about money. Her money. And sometimes it was about sex, which wasn't a problem at all. But now? With the gala so near and her plan working so well? The last thing she needed was Petey screwing things up.

"Hey," he said, coming into the living room, his large hands wrapped around a white bread sandwich. "You know that George Bush is coming to that party?"

"Yeah," she said, not caring one bit. But Petey liked his celebrities. Especially that Darcy Taylor. She was his favorite, and he drooled like a seventeen-year-old whenever he saw her picture. Janelle had heard the model was invited to the party. What she didn't know was whether she should tell Petey or wait and surprise him.

He took a huge bite of his sandwich, and a piece of lettuce fell to the carpet. He wouldn't pick it up. He never did. But why should she care? This place came with a maid. She'd have a maid in her new house, that's for sure. And a cook, and a driver, and hot and cold running pool boys.

She smiled. Petey took another bite. Something was up with him. But what?

"LADIES, GENTLEMEN, the sooner you take your seats, the sooner Ms. Taylor will make her statement."

Mitchell shifted a little to his right, almost behind the big pillar in the banquet-hall press-room. The place was packed with every kind of reporter, from those with network logos on their cameras to wild-haired youths typing on minuscule laptops.

Darcy Taylor was a news event. It had never struck him as forcefully as it did right now, he thought, watching the frenzy of excitement around him. It had never occurred to him that she was this big. Why would it? He'd never been one to cater to the media, and he rarely paid attention to celebrity news. When he saw Darcy's picture in magazines or in commercials, he never stopped to think about the ramifications of her position. But it was clear as crystal now that her retirement was a much bigger deal than he'd realized.

The man next to her on the dais looked as if he'd done this kind of thing hundreds of times. White-haired yet youthful-looking, he was deft with the pushy crowd, keeping a firm grip on things. Until there was absolute quiet, no one was going to ask even one question.

The silence rippled through the room, with only the sound of a cough, then the high trill of a cell phone, which was hushed instantly.

''Thank you. For those of you who don't know me, I'm Hank Fielding, Ms. Taylor's manager. We're going to make a brief announcement and then field some questions, but only for fifteen minutes. We're leaving in twenty minutes, period.''

He looked behind him, and through a door Mitch hadn't noticed, Darcy walked into the room. The flashbulbs went off like strafing fire, making him recoil, and no one was even turned his way. Darcy smiled. She smiled that million-dollar grin, as easy as you please, as if there were no cameras, no mikes. Jeez. He'd never seen anything like it. He felt as if she was smiling at him. Just at him. But she didn't know he was there. She certainly couldn't see him through this throng. But the phenomenon existed all the same. He felt a personal jolt of recognition and a totally irrational sense of pleasure as she stepped forward to the table. Maybe pleasure wasn't accurate. He felt special. Chosen. As if she'd singled him out.

He forced his gaze from her and looked around the room. Every face in the crowd had a similar expression. A kind of silly grin. Very much like the one he must have. Women, men, young, old, it didn't matter. They were all smitten, and from just one smile.

She was magic, that's all. Magic. The smile had power behind it, some strange voodoo that he'd never encountered before. It wasn't the same as when she was alone with him. This was a different sort of energy.

Hank cleared his throat, nodded once at Darcy, who sat with perfect grace behind a large table covered with microphones. "As of tomorrow morning at nine a.m. eastern time, Darcy Taylor will no longer represent Avelon Cosmetics or maintain contracts with any other cosmetics firms. She has officially announced her retirement and will no longer be accepting assignments in any medium."

A loud roar rose from the center of the room. Not a murmur. A murmur would have been understandable. This was a gasp, a cry from each member in the audience, and as Mitch studied face after face, he saw the same thing reflected—betrayal. But why? What did Darcy owe these strangers?

A dozen hands shot up in the air, but Hank didn't acknowledge them. "Ms. Taylor has bought a home here in Austin, where she intends to live quietly as a private citizen. She has no intention of starting a cosmetics firm of her own, or a modeling agency."

Three of the gesticulating hands came down. Ten more took their place.

"It is important to note that Ms. Taylor is not leaving Avelon because of any bad blood. In fact, Avelon has been incredibly generous and supportive of Ms. Taylor's decision to retire."

Low laughter cropped up around the room, but it didn't catch on.

"Ms. Taylor would also like it to be known that she is not retiring due to ill health." Hank looked at her, raised his right brow.

She nodded.

"Thank you, ladies and gentlemen," he said, stepping to the table. He stood behind Darcy, hovering over her left shoulder protectively.

The reporters were practically leaping out of their skin in an effort to get picked to ask the first question. Hank's assessing gaze traveled slowly over the pack. "Ginny."

"Darcy, are you having a baby?"

Hank opened his mouth, but Darcy stopped him with a shake of her head. She leaned into the sea of mikes. "No. I'm not."

"Are you trying?"

"No. I'm not."

Hands waving, shoving forward, the crowd was like a new creature made of hundreds of arms and legs.

"Fred."

"Fred Standard," the man said. "*Rolling Stone.* Darcy, there's a rumor that you and Richard Gere have been seeing each other for months now."

"That's news to me," she said. "And Mr. Gere."

"Is it true your ex-husband was abusive?"

"No, it is not true."

"Darcy, is it true you've been battling an eating disorder?"

"No, it is not true."

Hank looked over the crowd, and Mitch could see a shadow of annoyance cross his face. He whispered something to Darcy. She nodded, although her smile dimmed.

"Chelsea," he said.

Several heads turned toward the middle of the room, where Chelsea Markum held court. She nodded at her cameraman, touched a hand to her hair. "Darcy, is it true that you've retired so that you can have children, and that you've come to Austin to seek the services of Dr. Mitchell Maitland of the Maitland Maternity Clinic to help you with artificial insemination?"

Darcy's face reddened slightly, and he wondered if anyone who didn't know her would guess at her discomfort.

"No," she replied.

"Then are we to assume that you're trying to conceive in the natural way? With Dr. Maitland?"

"No," Darcy said again. She looked at Hank, and he stepped forward and pointed to a young man from CBS. He didn't get a chance to speak.

Chelsea wasn't finished yet. "Isn't it true that you and Mitchell Maitland spent last night together? Or was that someone else you were kissing in the driveway this morning?"

Darcy gave the woman a look that singed the air between them. "I was with my old friend Dr. Maitland, who was kind enough to let me stay with him when my own home had been overrun by reporters."

She nodded curtly at Hank. He held up both hands. "That's it, ladies and gentlemen. And Chelsea."

Laughter ended the session, but it didn't do anything for Chelsea Markum's mood. She looked daggers at Hank and Darcy, then turned to her cameraman again. As she talked to him, her gaze skirted the pillar Mitch stood behind, and he ducked back. After a few seconds, while he waited for her to turn, he headed toward the door. The last thing he wanted was to be seen here. Darcy had enough trouble without him butting in.

He shouldn't have come. But he was glad he did. He understood so much more about her now, and the problems she faced. If he could help in any way—

"Dr. Maitland."

The voice stabbed him in the back. Chelsea Markum. He'd been inches from a clean escape. He turned slowly.

The camera was already rolling. The reporter's smile was smug as hell. "Dr. Maitland. Would you please tell us what Darcy Taylor means to you?"

"She's an old friend," he said.

"You've known her for how long?"

"Since grade school."

"Was Darcy informed before she arrived that Maitland Maternity has been rocked by scandals in the last few months?"

"Excuse me," Mitch said, turning his back. There was no way he was going to engage in this joke of an interview. The best thing to do was keep his mouth shut and get the hell out.

"Dr. Maitland," she said, walking right behind him. "Isn't it true that there was a murder on the premises of Maitland Maternity just a month ago?"

He gritted his teeth. She knew damn well what had happened in that murder case, and everyone at Maitland had been exonerated.

"And isn't it true, Dr. Maitland, that someone claiming to be a family member abandoned a baby on the back steps of the clinic?"

He shoved a photographer out of his path, then headed straight toward the exit. The press followed him, like the wake of a ship, with Chelsea and her cameraman in the lead. It was too late to pretend Darcy wouldn't know he had come. She'd see it on the news, if she wasn't aware of it already.

Damn, he hadn't wanted this to turn into his circus. He'd come because he needed to understand, not interfere. But it didn't look like he had much choice.

He wasn't going to cooperate. Chelsea held up her mike once more, but before she had a chance to trip him with her skewed questions, Mitch got hold of the heavy door, and in a move he'd remember forever, shut it in her face.

He knew the door hadn't touched her, but it did do the trick. It gave him the chance to escape. By the time he'd reached the street, he was alone.

He wasn't foolish enough to believe it was over. He was going to have to face the press again, just as Darcy was. As long as he didn't hurt her or make things worse, then he was willing to do whatever it took. Interviews. Silence. He wasn't sure which would be better, but Hank would know.

For now, he needed to get back to the clinic and his real life. Where no one wanted his picture, and no one cared that he'd woken up next to the most beautiful woman in the world.

And that he wanted to wake up to her again tomorrow.

CHAPTER SEVENTEEN

DARCY CRINGED as she watched the tabloid show. She couldn't have cared less what they said about her, but they had focused on the local angle, the troubles with the Maitland Maternity Clinic, and especially Mitch.

She could feel his tension, even though they weren't touching. He'd been home only five minutes when he'd gotten the phone call from his secretary to turn on channel seven. A moment later, his life had spilled across the screen. The ultimate intruder, the unblinking eye that had taken her years to accept, was focused on Mitchell, and there wasn't a damn thing she could do about it.

"They could have used a more recent picture," he mumbled as he watched the screen with morbid fascination. "How do they know so much?"

"That's what they do," Darcy said. "They're like termites. They crawl into the woodwork. Into every crevice and dark corner."

A picture of Megan flashed on the screen, and it wasn't flattering. She looked haggard and worn, not at all her usual vibrant self.

"For God's sake." Mitchell gesticulated at the television. "We'd just found out that *Tattle Today* had put up a fifty-thousand-dollar reward to get an exclusive interview with the baby's mother. Some damn photographer took her picture at the worst time."

"Of course."

"Why do they do that?"

She shook her head. "I wish I knew. They say the public wants it. But I wonder if they'd demand such ugliness if it wasn't handed to them in daily doses."

His curse echoed her sentiments exactly. He turned to the set, to pictures of Beth and Ellie, to stock shots of the clinic. Next, there was videotape of him at the press conference, trying to escape. Then the show cut to her, the moment she'd spotted him in the crowd. Seeing her reaction floored her. Up to that moment, she'd had her public face squarely on. The trained smile that appeared to come from deep inside. The wide eyes that signified nothing. The practiced toss of her hair. It was all a facade. But the look on her face there, on the screen, was totally unguarded. For the first time she could remember, she'd left herself open. She'd taken off the only disguise that mattered.

She looked desperate. Anxious. Blatantly concerned. And because no good deed goes unpunished, the commentator, a blonde with a lisp as familiar to America as apple pie, raised her brow. "Darcy Taylor. Burned in romance once. Gone back home to this man. Dr. Mitchell Maitland."

Darcy's image faded, and in its place was a still photograph of another woman. When Mitch inhaled sharply, she knew exactly who it was.

"Married once before to his college sweetheart, Maitland had his own dark tragedy when both the wife of this fertility specialist and their infant died in childbirth.''

The blood drained from Darcy's face, making her feel faint. Mitch had hunched over as if he'd been slugged in the chest. The woman on television went on, speaking in a perfectly conversational tone, ripping the two of them to shreds sound bite by sound bite.

Darcy reached for the remote, but Mitch's cold hand caught hers. At least he stopped her trembling.

Angela's picture disappeared. The reporter, with her bright white perfect teeth, no hair out of place, and enough confidence to assure the most skeptical viewer that her words were gospel, turned to face Camera B. "Darcy Taylor. Supermodel. Entrepreneur. Reportedly one of the wealthiest women in America. But she has her own secrets, and they don't have anything to do with cosmetics.''

Darcy gasped as a picture of her father, years older than her memories, flashed on the screen.

"Roger Taylor. Sixty-four years old. Living in a trailer park in Reno, Nevada. The welfare recipient survives by using food stamps and eating several meals a week at the local shelter.''

They showed Darcy walking down the catwalk at a Versace show, wearing a million-dollar dress. Flashbulbs popped all around her like exploding stars. She looked like a woman who ate caviar and champagne for breakfast. Who wouldn't think twice about throwing her own father out the door, leaving him to struggle on the county's dime.

"Tomorrow, we'll bring you an exclusive interview with Roger Taylor. Stay tuned for Glen Parker and channel seven weather after this.''

Mitch turned to her, but she only saw him in shadow. She felt terribly cold. Her teeth chattered. She watched as a bright young thing extolled the virtues of some kind of tampon.

''Darcy?''

''Hmm?''

''Are you okay?''

''Sure,'' she said. The smile she'd practiced for a lifetime settled on her face. ''I'm just fine.''

''That was your dad?''

''Yeah.''

''Did you know he was living in—''

''No. I didn't. I haven't heard from my father in sixteen years.''

''At all?''

''No. My mother had some dealings with him, but she kept me in the dark about them. I think she gave him a divorce on the condition that he never contact us again.''

''And now?''

''Now, whatever my mother said or did is irrelevant. The fact that my father abandoned us is irrelevant. Anything resembling the truth is irrelevant.''

''You'll explain—''

She turned to Mitch. ''To whom? What am I going to say?''

''Start with the fact that the bastard deserted you.''

''You don't understand. I'm the villain in this skit. No amount of truth is going to change that.''

''I don't get it.''

''I know. And you shouldn't have to. I'm sorry.''

She stood, dislodging his hand. She'd forgotten it was there, and now it didn't matter. If she could just remember where she'd left her purse—

"Darcy? What are you doing?"

"Do you see my bag anywhere? It's black leather. Oh, wait, there it is." She grabbed the purse from beside the couch and dug for her keys.

"You're not leaving, are you?"

She nodded.

"Why?"

Her hand stilled. For a split second she thought about staying. But then reality came back. Her reality. Now his reality. "I've got to go."

He came up to her, put his hands on her arms. "No, you don't."

She faced him. She looked into his beautiful green eyes, right into the worry. There was no way she was going to do this to him. Not now. Maybe in five years, when she'd been out of the public eye for a long time. But not now. "I'll call you," she said.

"Don't. We can get through this. Together."

"Maybe we can. But we're not going to." She stepped out of his embrace. "I'm sorry, Mitch."

"For what?"

God, how she wanted to make things different. But they weren't different. This was her life, and she had to live it. The least she could do was protect those she cared about. But she knew if she said one word, if she looked at him for a second longer, she'd burst into tears.

In the single most difficult act of her life, she turned and walked to the front door. She opened it. She walked out. And she shut the door behind her.

It had been a nice fairy tale, ending up with Mitch in a pretty house with perfect children. But there wasn't going to be a happily ever after for her.

MITCH STARED at the closed door for a long time. He couldn't have said how long. He couldn't have said what he thought about. Too much information had hit him all at once, and he couldn't assimilate it. He felt as if he'd stumbled into quicksand, sinking helplessly into some dark place, leaving everything he knew behind.

He shouldn't have let her go. She needed him. Didn't she?

He wasn't sure. Damn it, he wasn't sure if Darcy needed him or not. How could that be? He'd known her most of his life, and this simple thing eluded him. His gaze moved to the television. A weather map shifted and changed to show the day's climate. What in hell had just happened here?

Angela. They'd talked about Angela. And they'd pointed out what so many others had been too polite to say: she'd died, their son had died because of him. Because he should have seen the signs of preeclampsia long before Angela had gotten into trouble. He should have insisted on a C-section. He should have known that her color wasn't good, that her insulin levels were off....

He should have saved her. But he hadn't. And he hadn't saved his son. The great Dr. Mitchell Maitland had botched the most important thing in his life. All his training hadn't been worth a damn thing. He hadn't saved them.

Darcy. He couldn't save her, either. No. There was

nothing he could do to the press. He was one man. Darcy was internationally famous, and nothing but time, and a long time, at that, would have any impact on the situation. She would be recognized in grocery stores, at gas stations, at the movies. People would nudge their friends and stare. They'd interrupt her conversations, ask for autographs, expect things from her. Expect her not to feel the weight of their adulation.

And what could he do? Hide her? Not Darcy. Pretend it didn't matter? It did. It mattered because of his family. The clinic. He couldn't put those things at risk. He wouldn't.

And now Darcy's father popped out of the woodwork. The son of a bitch changed Darcy's life, forced her into working before she'd even finished high school, and now he wanted his share. In a fair world, he would get just what he deserved. But it wasn't a fair world. Not by half.

Mitch went into the kitchen and made coffee. He had to count the spoons of ground beans four times until he got it right. His hand wasn't all that steady when he poured the water. When it was finally brewing, he sat at the table. His neck hurt. He rolled his head slowly, hearing a little pop but finding no relief. He needed a sauna and a massage. He needed—

Where had she gone? To her house? It would be swarming with reporters. To a hotel? Probably. What if he could find her? Bring her back?

No. She couldn't be safe here. Not with him.

THE LAST regular customer signed the credit card receipt. Shelby Lord gave him his copy. "Thank you. Come again."

The man grunted as he pushed open the door. Shelby waited a few seconds, then locked up, turning the Open sign to Closed. Sighing with relief after a tough day, she headed to booth four. Anna Maitland and Sara were sipping hot coffee and sharing a large slice of cheesecake. Shelby hoped there was still some left.

"You must have been terrified!"

Anna's voice sounded so earnest that Shelby knew she'd missed something important. She scooted into the booth across from Sara. "What happened?"

Sara recounted the night she'd nearly been killed. What got to Shelby the most was how calm Sara sounded. As if she were talking about a television show instead of her life.

"I called Ty Redstone. But there's not much he can do. I didn't get a license plate number, and it was too dark for me to see who was driving."

"This is too creepy," Shelby said. "I don't think you should stay at the rooming house anymore. You come stay with me."

Sara smiled and gave her hand a squeeze. "Thanks, Shelby, but no. I'm being very careful. And there are people staying at the rooming house, so I doubt very much anything will happen there."

"Okay, but there is one thing we can do. Take you off nights."

"That's not fair to the others."

Shelby nodded. "Right. You should work nights. And if you get killed, we'll write She Was Fair on your tombstone."

Anna rubbed her arms, and Shelby saw that even

though the temperature hadn't changed a degree, Anna had broken out in goose bumps.

"Okay," Sara said. "You win. For now."

"Thank you." Shelby got up, fetched the coffeepot and filled their mugs. The cheesecake on the plate was gone, so she got the rest of it and put it on the table. It was only half finished, but the way she was feeling, there wouldn't be a crumb left by the end of the night. Getting the creeps always made her hungry.

"Let's talk about something else," Sara said.

For a moment, they didn't speak at all. But that wasn't for lack of a subject. The cheesecake took priority. Once they'd each had several bites, Shelby remembered something. She turned to Anna. "Did Janelle ever get the paperwork on the baby's birth?"

Anna shook her head. "Evidently, the papers were destroyed in a fire, but they think they have microfiche records they can duplicate."

"So the baby is still at your mother's?"

"And she's loving every minute of it. I swear, if she could, I bet she'd have another baby in a heartbeat."

"I'd love to have a baby someday." Sara sighed.

Anna's cheeks got the tiniest bit pink.

"Anna? Do you have something to share?"

"I wish."

"You and me both," Shelby said. "But then, when would I have time to date, even if someone was interested?"

"Shelby, would you stop?" Anna took another bite of cheesecake. "When it's meant to happen, it will."

"Of course it will," Shelby said, but she didn't

believe it. She wasn't the type men liked in that way. They always wanted to be friends, which, she supposed, was better than nothing.

"Talking about no time," Sara said, "how go the plans for the gala?"

"Shockingly enough, things are going pretty smoothly. You won't believe the celebrities that are coming. George and Barbara Bush, Cybil Sheppard, Clint Black, Annie Potts, we hope Darcy Taylor…"

Shelby looked at Sara at the mention of Darcy's name.

"Have you two been talking to Beth?" Anna asked.

Sara nodded. "She's pretty convinced that Darcy and Mitch are an item."

"In fact," Shelby added, "she told me that Mitch is crazy in love with her, but he's not doing anything about it."

"I know," Anna said. "They were so close for so long. But I'm not sure…. I wonder if Mitch isn't being practical."

"Practical?" Sara sipped her coffee, made a face, then put a packet of sweetener in the mug. "How do you mean?"

"It can't be easy, being with a celebrity."

"But if he loves her…"

"Yeah. I guess. But I worry about him. He's so bright in some ways, but when it comes to relationships, he can be such a guy."

"Isn't that the truth," Shelby said. "They all can be such *guys*."

"I wonder, though, if he's ever really gotten over Angela's death." Anna stared at her hands for a moment. "It's time, if he hasn't. He needs to get on with life, and I guess if Darcy is his reason to do that, then he should go for it, no matter what."

"Sometimes," Shelby said, "getting on with life is the hardest thing of all."

"Yeah," Sara said. "Especially when you don't know what kind of life you're supposed to get on with."

Shelby and Anna turned to Sara. "You'll get through this," Anna said.

"And we'll be right beside you when you do," Shelby added.

Anna's hand went to the middle of the table. Shelby put her hand on top of it. Sara blinked a few times, as if she were trying hard not to cry. Then she put her hand on the pile. It was good to have friends, Shelby thought. Very good, indeed.

DARCY PICKED UP the phone at the fourth ring. She knew who it was. He'd been calling her for five days now. She hadn't been able to answer until today. Until her decision had been made.

"Hey, Maitland," she whispered into the receiver.

"Hey, Taylor."

Oh, his voice. His deep velvet voice. She'd dreamed the sound, but she realized the dream had been way off.

"I've been trying to reach you."

"I know. I'm sorry. I should have just talked to you. But...I don't know. I don't seem to be very rational right now."

"I understand."

"Do you?"

He paused, but she could hear his even breathing. "I think so. What I'm trying to figure out is what I can do about it."

"Mitch, there's nothing—"

"Wait," he said, interrupting her. "That's not what I want to talk to you about."

She sighed as she settled onto her couch. The plastic covering squeaked with her weight, reminding her yet again of what she was giving up. "What did you call for?"

"The gala is tomorrow night."

"I know. It's pretty hard to miss all the publicity about it."

"Darcy, come with me. Screw all of them. Just come with me, and then, after, we can figure out what to do."

She opened her mouth to say yes. But no sound came out. Her throat tightened, and her eyes filled with tears. She'd never cried more in her life than this past week. She'd wept until she thought she'd dried up inside. But she hadn't. Hearing his voice, his simple request, made her weep again. "Mitch, it's no good."

"What's no good? The publicity? Who gives a damn? We'll get through it."

"Things have gone from bad to worse here," she told him, "My father is talking to every reporter he can find."

"Hasn't anyone figured out that he abandoned you?"

"No one seems to care much about that. Except me, of course."

"We'll get through it."

"If I thought it was that easy…"

"It is. We're making it more complicated than it has to be. If we just take it one step at a time, we'll be fine."

"How can you say that? Haven't you been paying attention?"

"To the news? Screw 'em."

She laughed at his audacity. "Mitch, they're never going to leave us alone."

"That's not true."

"Right. You're right. In all seriousness, I think they will forget about us after a couple of years if something else doesn't happen—say, a pregnancy by artificial insemination."

"Don't say that. It looks bleak now, but things will get better. I swear to God, Darcy. I don't want to lose you again."

"You won't. But I think it's best that we remain friends."

"After the night we spent together, you can go back to being friends?"

No. She couldn't. But she was going to try. She had to. Because the alternative was to lose him forever. "Sure I can. That's what we are. That's what we've always been. And when things calm down…"

"Things will never calm down."

Her throat tightened again, making it hard to breathe. She struggled for a moment, willing herself not to sob. When she was in control, she pasted on her patented smile. "Mitch, it's been incredible seeing you again. I'm sorry it had to go this way, but really, there hasn't been much harm done. I have to go."

"No. Please, Darcy. No."

She waited for the only words that had a chance of changing her mind. The silence built to a crescendo. The words didn't come. She'd known they wouldn't. "Goodbye, Maitland."

"Darcy."

She hung up the phone. Closed her eyes and struggled not to fall apart. It had to be this way. She'd walked into his life like Typhoid Mary, causing havoc everywhere she turned. He didn't deserve that. No one did.

And yet...

There was still a part of her that wanted to believe things could work out. She'd thought the years had killed that part of her. The dreamer. The idealist. But Mitch had awakened the sleeping giant.

It was foolish to think about a life with Mitch. More than foolish.

She turned until she faced the kitchen. Hank sat at the table, his pen poised above the contract to sell the house. "Hold it," she said. Even as the words came out, she knew she'd pay. But she couldn't leave. Not yet.

CHAPTER EIGHTEEN

THE CHAMPAGNE was bitter. Mitchell put his glass down at the waiter's station and headed for one of the four bars set up in the huge hotel banquet room. By the time he reached the bartender, he'd admitted to himself that it wasn't the champagne that was bitter. It was him. He didn't want to be here. He didn't want to hear the laughter, the sounds of the orchestra, receive the congratulations. He wanted Darcy, and he couldn't have her.

"Scotch and soda," he said, then watched as the bartender, who was exceptionally attractive, poured. He thanked her, left a five-dollar tip and headed out to look for a quiet corner, if there was such a thing to be found at the gala.

Twenty-five years. That was a long run in anyone's book. The clinic had been as much a part of his life as his siblings had been, as much an influence on him as his parents. He'd been nine the day it opened. Darcy had been with him at the ribbon cutting. She'd gotten them both in hot water by sneaking off with several glasses of champagne. He'd hated the taste, but he didn't tell her that. He'd wanted her to think he was an old hand at drinking. That it was no big thing.

His mother had found them hours later, drunk as

skunks, hiding in the catering tent. He'd been grounded for a long, long time. But that didn't bother him at all. He liked spending time alone. What had smarted was that he'd been forbidden to see Darcy for two weeks.

He realized a lady was smiling at him, and he smiled back, trying to place her. A patient? Maybe. Or one of Beth's friends? Damn, she looked familiar. He hated it when he couldn't remember someone's name.

"How are you?" he said when it was apparent she wasn't going to let him off the hook.

"Very well, thank you. This is a wonderful party."

"Yeah, yeah. It is."

She smiled again, and he noticed her teeth, which was an odd thing to notice. But they were so perfect. In fact, everything about her was perfect, if tiny. He was afraid to ask her anything, because he obviously knew her.

"I admire the work that's done here," she said. "Nothing's more important than children."

He nodded. "They can make the difference, can't they?"

"Absolutely."

The silence stretched, and just as Mitch decided to ask her if he could get her some hors d'oeuvres, a good-looking man joined the lady, putting his hand on her arm in a gesture of ownership Mitch recognized immediately.

He smiled politely at Mitch, then turned to his companion. "Can I get you something to eat, Vanna?"

Mitch mentally slapped his forehead. No *wonder* she looked familiar. Vanna White. Duh.

"It was nice talking to you," she said to him, smiling again. Then she and her friend, probably her husband, wandered toward the food.

He shook his head. Next time someone smiled at him, he would try to leave before he made an ass of himself.

Someone tapped him on the shoulder, and he turned to see Beth. Her cheeks were a little flushed, her eyes wide. "You look spectacular," he said.

"Thank you. You look like hell."

"Thanks."

"It's true, and you know it. You're miserable and you're not even trying to hide it."

"You're right."

"Tonight isn't about us. It's about Mother. So don't make her worry, okay?"

"Yes, Beth. I'll be good."

"Besides, there's no law that says you can't have a good time, even if she isn't here."

"She?" he said innocently.

"Oh, please. Tell it to someone who doesn't have a brain."

"I just wish she'd come," he confessed. "I wish I'd handled things differently."

Beth's face changed as she focused on him. Her gaze caught his and didn't waver. "Mitchell, are you in love with her?"

He opened his mouth, intending to say no. But he couldn't. "I don't know," he said. "I honest to God don't."

"Well, don't you think it's important to figure it out?"

"How? She's leaving. She doesn't want us to be anything more than friends."

Beth's grin came back as she shook her head. "You're such a *guy*. I can't even believe it."

"What does that mean?"

"It means that when it comes to love, you're clueless. Absolutely."

"Thanks."

"Don't mention it."

"So? Are you going to enlighten me?"

"Listen, big brother. The woman came back here for a reason, and it wasn't about the house or about wanting to have a baby. She came back for you."

"She did not."

"No?"

He shook his head. "She came back because of the clinic."

Beth laughed. Really laughed. When she was through, she wiped her eyes with her fingertips. "God, Mitch, buy a clue."

"So you're saying I should go after her?"

"Yes. I'm saying you should go after her."

"Oh."

His sister shook her head in despair. "Men. It's amazing you can tie your own shoes."

Mitch hardly heard the insult. He was too busy digesting this radical theory of Beth's. Could Darcy want him to follow her? Could she be waiting now, the way she'd waited in the park all those years ago?

HER COAT POCKETS were getting full. No wonder, with five bottles of Dom Perignon stuck in the hidden flaps. Janelle had debated bringing the fake fur, but then she figured at this shindig, everyone would be wearing furs. Still, she could probably fit one more bottle in the back pocket. She intended to take everything she could, one way or another. It served them right for being so friggin' ostentatious.

She walked out of the coat room, smiled innocently at the attendant, and grabbed another glass of bubbly. Then she scanned the room, looking for Petey. He was having a high time. Dancing and drinking. It was like the old days, only back then, they danced to a jukebox and they drank whiskey. Say what you wanted to about Petey, he knew how to party.

She turned, almost bumping into Clint Black. He had his arm around his pretty wife, Lisa Hartman Black. God, what a pair. They were both so good-looking. Janelle smiled, and Clint smiled back.

See? She fit right in. This was the kind of crowd she'd always belonged in. Once Lacy was out of the picture and she'd gotten the phony paperwork squared away, she'd move to Beverly Hills. She'd shop on Rodeo Drive and buy any damn thing her heart desired. Diamonds, big fat ones. Furs, real ones. Everything she'd always deserved.

Damn, that was Cybil Sheppard talking to Ellie. She was taller than Janelle had thought, but a damn fine-looking woman. And there was Barbara Bush! Not wearing her little pearls tonight. Man, she'd stood the test of time.

Janelle chugged the rest of the champagne and headed for the food tables. Crab legs, shrimp the size of her fist, oysters, three different kinds of caviar. They could keep the sushi. Ugh. She loaded her plate, then turned to watch the dance floor as she ate.

Petey was dancing with Anna Maitland. No doubt talking about the wedding. Maybe she'd invite Clint and Lisa. They seemed like such a nice couple.

She took a bite of shrimp as the song ended. Petey took hold of Anna's hand and headed her way. By the time they got through the crowd, Janelle had finished the seafood and given her plate to a passing waiter.

"Janelle! You look so beautiful!"

"Thanks, Anna. So do you. And the party is fantastic. You've done a wonderful job."

"With a lot of help," Anna said, smiling broadly. "I think I'll stick to weddings, though. I'm just so glad the hard part is over. Everyone came, did you see? The Bushes are here, and Willie Nelson and, oh, so many celebrities!"

"All because of you," Janelle said.

"Oh, no. It's not. It's because of Mother. People respect her so."

"Of course they do," Janelle said, her smile starting to ache. It was getting harder and harder to put on the act for these people.

"You realize that come next week, we have to sit down and do some serious planning. It takes time to make a perfect wedding, and that's what I want you to have."

"Thanks, hon. I'll make sure to call. We can have lunch or something."

"Terrific." Anna turned toward the dance floor and knocked into a beautiful blonde Janelle didn't recognize.

"Anna Maitland?"

Anna didn't recognize her, either, from the look on her face.

"I'm Caroline Lamont."

The name must have meant something to Anna. Her eyes got wide as saucers.

"I don't know if you've heard, but Austin Cahill and I are engaged."

"Oh?" Anna said, only it came out more like a squeak than a word.

"Yes. And we'd like to know if you'd be available to coordinate our wedding. It won't be until next August, but we'd like to get started on the plans. I know you're booked well into next year, but is there any chance?"

"I'm sure we can work something out."

"Wonderful. I know you put this little shindig together, and I must say you've done a remarkable job. I think Austin was right to suggest you."

"Austin suggested me?"

Caroline nodded. "Speak of the devil. He's waiting for me. Poor dear can't figure out what to do if I'm not right at his side. I'll call you."

"Okay," Anna said.

It was all Janelle could do not to burst out laughing. Anna looked as if the rug had been pulled out from beneath her feet. In fact, she didn't look like a woman who'd just gotten a plum job at all. She seemed stunned. Bewildered.

A mystery! Janelle loved nothing better. She decided to find out what the deal was with Austin, Caroline Lamont and pretty little Anna Maitland. In the meantime, she'd just take another glass of champagne and maybe one more shrimp.

MITCH EAVESDROPPED as he nursed his drink. Anna, Abby, Ellie and Beth huddled together near the dance floor with their friend Katie Carrington, gossiping about the guests. Mitchell couldn't have cared less about the conversation, except that it kept him from thinking his own thoughts. He had to make a decision, and he had to do it tonight. Most of all, he had to make sure he wasn't acting selfishly. Well, not entirely selfishly. The *most* important thing was Darcy's happiness. But if they could be together...

"She still doesn't have the birth certificate," Beth said.

Katie nodded.

"I know. What's that about?"

"From what I hear," Abby whispered, "the records were destroyed in a fire."

"But surely there's a way to get a duplicate?"

"Yeah. There is." Ellie grabbed a glass of champagne from a passing waiter. "And she's working on it. It's a shame, though. It's obvious how much she loves the baby and how it's hurting her to be apart from him, even for a little while."

Beth shook her head. "I can't imagine being away from my baby for even two seconds."

Anna swung around to face her sister. "You're not...?"

"No. At least, I don't think so."

"Oh, Beth," Abby said. "Wouldn't that be something?"

Mitch headed away from the group of women. It wasn't even nine o'clock yet, so he couldn't leave. Or could he? Who would miss him?

Because the gods had a sense of humor, the next

person he laid eyes on was Megan. She was standing with Connor O'Hara. Abby's husband, Kyle, R.J. and Shelby stood around her, listening to her intently. Although Mitch couldn't hear her over the strains of "It Had to Be You," he knew it was a funny story. Not just because of the smiles, but because of the mischief in his mother's eyes.

A moment later, the laughter came, and Mitch made the decision to leave. He couldn't do this any longer. He had to think.

He put his drink down, and as he was about to head out, Megan caught his attention. She gave him an enigmatic grin, then she slowly turned her head until she faced the elevator.

His heart beating like a drum, he started walking, his vision blocked by partygoers. He bumped into Annie Potts, whom he'd met on several occasions, but after a very brief apology, he darted past her.

There. That shoulder. It was her. *Darcy had come.*

Despite what she'd said, she'd come. He didn't run, even though he wanted to. He walked very, very fast until he saw her clearly.

She was the most beautiful creature he'd ever seen—a vision in a scarlet strapless dress, with her hair a swirl of curls atop her head. His heart ached as he looked at her. She was far more than stunning. There weren't words, at least not for a scientist like him. Poets would have no trouble finding something to say.

She had been looking around. Looking for him. When he caught her gaze, she smiled. He laughed, feeling seventeen again.

He reached her a moment later. They didn't speak.

Not at first. He just looked at her, and she looked back. The only two people in the universe.

But the solitude didn't last. It ended with the flash of a camera. A shout of her name. A flurry of activity as the press moved in on them.

Mitch wasn't willing to share.

He grabbed her hand and headed toward the kitchen. Twice, they were almost stopped, and twice, Mitch found an alternate route. Faster and faster he led her, and she kept up with every step.

He pushed open the swinging door to the kitchen and nearly bowled over a waiter carrying canapés. The man managed to save the platter, but Mitch didn't stick around to congratulate him. He kept walking past the ovens, past the sinks, past the surprised chef, until he found the door that led to the hallway. From there, he pulled Darcy along until he found what he was looking for. Steps to the roof.

He shut the door behind Darcy. The quiet came over them like a shawl, warm and comfortable and private. Just the sounds of the city far below.

He caught his breath after their dash through the hotel and when his pulse had settled, he smiled at his lady friend. "Hey, Taylor."

"Hey, Maitland."

"I'm awfully glad you could make it."

She grinned. "It was this or clean the refrigerator."

"Liar."

She nodded. "You're right. It was this or wonder forever if I'd made a mistake."

"Have you?"

"I don't know."

He touched her arm. He ran his fingertips down

slowly until he touched her fingers, then he squeezed her hand gently. "I don't know, either. But tell you what, let's not worry about it tonight. Okay? Let's just be here. With each other."

She nodded. And then she took two steps. Right into his arms.

He held her close, loving the feel of her against him. The smell of her hair made him dizzy with want, and the silk of her skin made him just plain crazy.

"Can you hear that?"

"What?"

"The orchestra. They're playing Cole Porter."

He grew still, listening. The music came floating up to him somehow. Faint, but definitely there. He thought about another time he'd been at a big party like this, with a band and all the trimmings. The prom. The prom Darcy had missed.

He let go his hold, but only to shift position. His right hand slid to the small of her back. His left hand lifted her hand about even with their shoulders.

She tilted her head, understanding his intent, but clearly curious. She wouldn't be for long.

After a deep breath, he began to dance. The hand behind her back signaled each move, and she followed as if they'd been dancing for a lifetime. The music grew louder as he twirled her around the black tar roof. The moon was their spotlight, and the stars glittered in four-four time.

Her smile deepened, and after he spun her under his arm, she laughed out loud. He joined her, glad to be alive but even more glad to be with her.

And then the song ended.

Mitch pulled her close once more, and this time, he kissed her.

She fairly melted in his embrace. She sighed as her arms went around his neck. It was perfect.

Later, he wasn't sure if it had been minutes or hours, she pulled back and smiled at him. "I thought you said you couldn't dance?"

"I couldn't."

"What do you call what we just did?"

"That? That was nothing."

"Oh?"

He shook his head. "Tonight, I could probably fly without an airplane, too."

"Come on, Maitland. Fess up. You know how to dance."

"All right. You caught me. I took some lessons."

"When?"

"About two months before you left."

"Really?" She looked so surprised. So delicious. The moonlight made her skin glow and her eyes light with fire.

"Hey. We were supposed to go to the prom together, remember? I didn't want to embarrass you."

"But you said you wouldn't dance with Elizabeth."

"That's right."

"Why not? You'd taken the lessons."

He nodded. "I didn't have the right dance partner."

"Oh, Mitch." She kissed him hard. Then looked at him again. "*This* is my prom," she whispered. "It's everything I ever wanted it to be."

"I don't have flowers for you."

She touched his face with the back of her hand. "Don't be silly. You've given me the moon."

CHAPTER NINETEEN

DARCY rested her head on the curve of Mitch's neck. Tired, happy and a little tipsy from the champagne, she tried to remember a night she'd enjoyed more.

Dancing on the rooftop.

She'd felt like Ginger to Mitch's Fred. He'd charmed her with his humor, his poise and his kisses. In fact, she wasn't sure he knew it yet, but she was a sure thing.

Silently urging the limo to go faster, she ran her hand under his tuxedo jacket, loving the warmth of his body beneath his shirt.

Like Cinderella, she knew this state of grace was going to be brief. That tomorrow, the real world would come to the fore. But at least she'd have tonight.

He sighed, and she felt him gently stroke her arm. She looked up just as he looked down. The kiss was as natural as breathing, as healing as a magic elixir. Her eyes fluttered closed as she focused on his taste, his scent.

"You sure this guy knows where he's going?" Mitch whispered.

"Yes."

"You think if I gave him a twenty he'd go faster?"

She grinned. "Impatient, are we?"

"Nah. Just want to go home and check the hockey scores."

"Is it hockey season?"

His laughter made his chest vibrate. "I have no idea."

"Oh, Maitland," she said, sighing with pleasure.

"Yeah. I know."

"It was much better than the prom."

"I'll say. There weren't any teachers hovering."

"No horrible fruit punch."

"No Phil Jasper with his wet willies and nuclear wedgies."

Darcy had forgotten about him. "What an obnoxious kid he was. Wonder what he's doing now?"

"He's the attorney general."

She lifted her head to look at him. "You lie."

"I don't. He's the attorney general for the state of Texas."

"Phil Jasper?"

"Uh-huh."

"Oh, heaven help us." She rested her head again. "What has the world come to?"

"It's chaos. Madness."

"But one has hope," she said. "For the future, I mean."

"Hmm. I'm very hopeful about the immediate future." He kissed the top of her head. "In fact, I'm downright thrilled about it."

Darcy sat up and looked out the tinted windows of the limo. "We're almost there."

"Excellent."

She smiled brightly. "So, should I just tell the driver to take you right home?"

"You do, and there'll be hell to pay."

She tried to look worried. "Hell to pay? Uh-oh. Guess you'd better stay at my place."

"Guess I'd better."

She smiled.

He smiled.

The limo stopped just in time.

MEGAN MAITLAND took one last look around the banquet room. The guests had gone, but the activity hadn't stopped. At least ten men and women scurried around, clearing dishes, picking up napkins, taking down decorations. She felt as though she was in the middle of a busy beehive and she was the very tired queen bee.

It had gone well. William would have been proud. Not just of the clinic that held his name, but of his children.

R.J. was a fine man, and he'd found himself a woman who would stand up to him when she needed to but who respected him tremendously.

Anna had her son, Will, and a thriving business as a wedding consultant.

Ellie had found Sloan, and with him had come a whole new family and a new way of life. Megan had never seen her daughter happier.

Kyle McDermott had finally won Abby's hand, and it had changed both of them for the better.

Beth had recovered from that nasty business with her ex-fiancé, and who would have guessed she'd have fallen so hard for Ty Redstone? He was someone William would have liked a great deal.

Jake... Well, Jake was still the mystery man. Who knew what his life would bring him?

And as for Mitch? She'd seen him with Darcy. Seen the look in his eye, the love that was so evident that everyone could see it but him. She'd also seen Darcy, and she knew that if they could just get past their fears, they would bring each other tremendous joy. They needed each other, and it was hard for her not to interfere. But she'd learned a lot these past few months. As difficult as it was, she had to let her children make their own choices and face their own demons, if need be.

Of course, she still had some demons of her own to face. Connor, the son she'd lost so long ago, back in her life as if by a miracle. Chase, her grandchild. So beautiful she wept at the thought of his cherubic face. Janelle, soon to be a part of this crazy, wonderful family of hers.

She was the luckiest woman on earth, so why was it that she woke up night after night with a knot of fear in her stomach? What was her subconscious trying to tell her?

William, she prayed silently, *show me. I'm not seeing things clearly. Please, my darling husband, I need your help. Something is dreadfully wrong. I feel it in a way only you would understand. What is it? What is it?*

MITCH BREATHED greedily, filling his lungs with air. He heard Darcy doing the same. In fact, the way he was lying on top of her, his chest touching hers, it had to be harder for her to gain her equilibrium. He didn't want to, but he rolled sideways, landing on the bed.

The rhythm of her gasps changed, and he knew he'd done a noble thing, a sacrifice right up there with giving a friend the shirt off his back or leaving the last piece of cherry pie. His consolation was that they still touched. And when he put his hand on her flat tummy, he felt even better.

"Holy cow," she said.

"You can say that again."

"Holy cow."

He grinned. "Didn't know I had it in me."

"No, I had it in me," she whispered wickedly, "and I knew it."

He smiled. "You're a devil. A devil with curly hair."

"That's true. I am."

"Thank God."

She laughed, and the sound was like music.

He closed his eyes, so content that it had to be a crime. "I'm glad you came to the party."

"Me, too. It was the most fun I've had since, well, just now."

"You know, of course, that despite our trip to the roof, the press is going to have a field day."

"Yes. I know it. I just hope they concentrate on me and not you."

"I don't care."

She was quiet for a while. Then she touched his hair. "You don't care now. But you will."

"No, I won't."

She sighed. "Oh, Mitch, you don't understand."

"I do. And I don't care. Whatever they throw at us, we'll survive. Eventually, they'll go away."

"True, but only after they've sucked us dry. And it's not just you and me. It's the rest of your family. The clinic."

"It doesn't matter. After these past few months—"

Her fingertips touched his lips, stilling his protest. "Mitch, I came to the party last night to say goodbye."

He sat up, dislodging her hand. "How can you mean that? After what we went through last night and this morning?"

"It's not easy," she said, but she didn't look him in the eye.

"So don't."

"Please. I have to."

"Why? Damn it, why?"

"Because there's too much at stake."

"Are you going to explain that?"

She sat up, punched the pillow behind her, then leaned back. The comforter and sheet lay bunched at her waist. His gaze went to her naked torso, to the incredible beauty of her breasts. But he forced himself to tear his gaze away. Now wasn't the time.

"Things are…complicated," she said.

He waited, saying nothing. He watched the dilemma play across her face, and he wondered, not for the first time, if he was making a mistake, pressing her like this. And yet, wasn't being with her the best thing he'd ever felt? Wasn't being inside her the safest place on earth?

"I've decided," she said finally, "that I'm not going to go ahead with the artificial insemination."

"Darcy—"

She held up her hand to quiet him. "I wasn't finished. I'm not going to do the AI, but I am completely determined to have a child. The natural way."

A pit of fear opened in his stomach the second she uttered the words. For a moment, he wasn't with Darcy at all, but Angela. Angela, the life bleeding out of her as she struggled to have their child the natural way.

His thoughts were interrupted by the look on Darcy's face. She looked as sad as he'd ever seen her. Disappointment took the color from her. Weariness made her eyes dull. Why? What was going on?

"I'm going back to New York," she said. "I'm going to find myself a nice guy. I don't know how, but I will."

"A nice guy?"

She nodded. "No one in show business, no one in the spotlight. Just a nice guy who'll be a good father to our child."

"Why New York?" He took a deep breath, then, before he lost his courage, he said, "Why not me?"

Her smile didn't make him feel any better. "Because I saw your face, sweetie. You don't want to have a child. The thought scares you to death."

"That's not true," he protested, even though he knew she wasn't completely off the mark. She didn't understand—

"It might not be true always, but it is now."

"Can't you...wait?"

"No. I can't. I've waited for sixteen years to have my own life. If it can't be just as I pictured it, then so be it. But it will be mine, and I will have babies. I don't need to make your life a mess in the process.''

"Wait a minute. You're presuming a hell of a lot.''

"Maybe so. But I'm right. I know I'm right. And no amount of wishful thinking is going to change that. Time might.''

"Time *will*.''

"No. Time might.''

"So that's it? You're out of here? We're history? It's the babies, come hell or high water?''

She cringed, and he wanted to take back his words. ''I might have said it a little more delicately, but yes. I came here for a reason, Mitch. I wanted to go back to the way things were. But we can't go back, can we?''

"We can sure as hell try.''

"But I did discover that my decision is a sound one. I look at your mother and see all her children around her, and I know that's what I want.''

He didn't know what to do. What to say. He wanted to force her to stay, to keep her here no matter what it took, but then...

He leaned against the headboard, staring at the empty wall across from them. ''I don't know why I didn't see it,'' he said, his voice hoarse as he said the words that had been inside him for so long. ''I didn't see it, and I was trained to see it. That's what I do. I save women's lives all the time. Save their children. I spot rare conditions. I change the very makeup of their bodies so they can bear their children. And she died. The baby died. Right there, when I was in the room. When I was supposed to be helping them.''

"Mitch, it wasn't your fault.''

"You don't know that."

"Yes, I do."

"How? You weren't there."

"I don't have to have witnessed the event to know that you're not God. No matter how much you'd like to think you are."

"Oh, come on, Darcy. It's not about playing God. It's about skill and training and observation. Things a first-year resident should have seen."

"Were you Angela's obstetrician?"

"No."

"Who was?"

"Stanley Elgin."

"Now, even I've heard of him. Isn't he an expert in his field?"

"Yes."

"Then why didn't he catch it?" she whispered. "He was her doctor."

"He didn't catch it because he assumed I would. I was her husband, for pity's sake. I was with her all the time."

"Okay. You win. You should have seen it. You should have saved her and your child. So now what?"

He turned to face her, shame and anger swirling inside him, making it hard to understand what she was saying.

"Now what? Is it a life sentence? Or is there a statute of limitations on beating yourself up?"

He had no idea what to say to her. She clearly didn't—

Darcy threw back the covers and got out of bed. "I'm going to put on the coffee," she said.

He watched her turn. Walk to the closet, get out

her robe and slip it on. Then he watched as she walked out of the room, leaving him alone with his thoughts. With his memories.

AT NINE-FIFTEEN, just after Darcy had poured Mitch his first cup of coffee, the phone rang. The only person who knew the number was Hank, and he rarely got up before eleven. Even as she picked up the receiver, she knew something was wrong.

"Hey, sweetheart," Hank said. His tone told her her instincts had been right on target.

"What is it?"

He sighed. Mitch put his cup on the table without taking a sip, his eyes worried.

"It's your father."

Her first thought was to say she had no father, but that wasn't true, was it?

"He's suing you."

"*What?*"

"I got the papers today. He's suing you for ten million dollars."

"You've got to be kidding. On what grounds?"

"Estrangement, abandonment and misuse of funds."

She had to sit down. "Abandonment? Like *I* left him?"

"I know." Hank's voice was low and even, meant to calm her down. But she had no intention of being calmed down.

"It's ridiculous. Isn't there some way to cut this off at the pass? Talk to a judge or something?"

"You know as well as I do that anyone can sue

anyone for anything. It doesn't matter if it's legitimate. We've been through this before."

"This is different."

"I know, hon."

"Do me a favor, will you, Hank? Try and get him to meet with me."

"Are you sure you want to do that?"

"Yes. I want to look him in the eyes."

"I'll do my best."

"Thanks."

"What do you want to do about the sale of the house?"

She looked at Mitch. His concern for her was genuine. It would be easy to delude herself into believing she could have a normal relationship with him. That the fame didn't matter, that the press would leave them be. But it wasn't true, and she knew it. She loved him too much to bring him into the circus of her life. If nothing else had convinced her, this phone call had. Her own father was suing her. If it wasn't so damn tragic, it would have been funny.

"Go ahead with it," she said.

"Are you sure?"

"Yes."

"Okay, kiddo. I'll call you later."

When she hung up the phone and turned to Mitch, she felt on the verge of tears. It had all gone so wrong. The dream she'd kept safe and close to her heart for all these years had fallen apart inch by inch until there was nothing left.

CHAPTER TWENTY

MITCH LISTENED carefully as Darcy told him about her father's lawsuit. He forced himself to stay cool and not let his building anger show. The last thing Darcy needed was for him to go off on a tear.

But that didn't mean he wasn't going to do something. His family had a top law firm on retainer. They'd been busy in the past few months, and now it appeared they were going to be busier. No way was he going to let Darcy's father put her through the wringer. The bastard had broken her heart all those years ago, and Mitch wasn't going to stand by and watch that happen again.

"It just doesn't seem possible, does it?" She tightened the sash of her robe and hugged herself. It was such a plaintive move. She was trying to protect herself in the only way she knew how.

"Hey, Taylor?"

Her smile was so weak, he knew she didn't mean it. "Yeah, Maitland?"

"Let me help."

Her brows went up. "What can you do?"

"First, we have lawyers on retainer. I can make one phone call—"

She shook her head, dismissing the idea.

"Why not?"

"It's not your problem. I've got an attorney, and believe me, he's paid plenty."

Mitch winced at his foolishness. Of course she had an attorney. She probably had a whole fleet of them standing at the ready. She didn't need his help. "Right, of course." He glanced at the clock. "I've got to get to the hospital. I've got rounds today."

"Sure."

"Listen, I'm gonna be at the hospital until at least five. But after that, we can go to dinner or something."

"Tell you what, let's talk later. I'm not sure what's going on today. I need to check with Hank—"

"Right. I'll, uh, go get dressed."

She nodded. He waited to see if she might say something else. But she didn't. All she did was stare at her coffee mug. He walked away, filled with defeat and sadness.

It was over. Just as quickly as it had begun. But at least this time they'd done it to each other. There'd been no outside interference. It was over, and it was stupid to think it could have ended any differently. She'd grown out of this town, whether she realized it or not. It never worked when people tried to go back to the old ways, to the people who once mattered.

He wished he hadn't made love with her. Because that had been better than anything he'd ever imagined. And better than anything he could hope to find again.

It would have been easier if she'd never come home. The old memories had stopped hurting years before. These new memories? He didn't want to think about them.

He hoped she'd be happy. That she'd find her nice guy, have a whole house full of kids. That the press would leave her be.

Man, it would have been something, though. It would have really been something.

"HONEY, there's nothing says you need to do this."

Darcy smiled at Hank. He was such a mother hen. Thank goodness. She'd needed a mother all these years. Boy, when they'd passed out perfect parents, she must have been standing in the wrong line. No, she wasn't going to do that. She had no business feeling sorry for herself. Not with all she had in life. Not with the gifts she'd been given. "I need to do this, Hank. It's not for him. It's for me."

Hank shook his head, and she noticed the dark circles under his eyes. She hadn't realized how old he'd gotten. To her, he'd just been Hank. But he must be close to retirement age, if not past it already.

When he left, she'd have no one. For real. But then, she was used to standing on her own two feet, wasn't she?

"He's in the back booth," Hank said. "And he seems damn nervous. I know he's tired from flying all night."

"Well, I'm damn nervous and tired, too. Wish me luck."

"You got it."

"I'll call you later."

"You don't want me to stick around?"

"Nope. Go home. It's Sunday. Relax. Watch TV. Read a book."

"Now you're just talking crazy."

She laughed, which felt damn good. Then she kissed him on his cheek and watched as he walked to his rented Mercedes. She waved, and then he was gone, and she had no more excuses.

She took a deep breath, turned and walked inside the coffee shop.

It was pretty crowded, but then it was Sunday, and people liked to go out for breakfast on Sunday. She adjusted her baseball cap and sunglasses, not wanting to be recognized. Not here.

She headed toward the back booths, and then she saw him.

Her heart stopped in her chest. It really was her father. Older—God, so much older—but it was him. He'd lost a lot of hair, gained a lot of weight. He was a parody of the man she'd adored as a young girl.

It was hard to keep walking. To face him. Because as she got closer, she saw all his mistakes right there on his face. Sallow complexion, red blotchy nose from too much alcohol. His hands shook as he tugged on a cigarette.

When she got to the booth, he looked up. His eyes were bloodshot; the deep blue she remembered had faded into a pale, watery gray. She wanted to weep.

"Darcy?"

She nodded, then sat opposite him.

He smiled awkwardly, showing discolored teeth. "You always wear those dark glasses?"

She took them off and folded them into her purse. "No, I don't."

"That's better. You look good. Real good."

"Thanks."

He laughed. She knew it was from nerves. It was

hard to look at him, but she didn't turn away. Facing him, facing everything head-on was what she had to do. Facing the fact that Mitchell wasn't going to be hers. Facing the fact that she couldn't have her little house in Austin. Facing the truth about the life she'd lived and the life she had in front of her. No more dreams. Dreams just made things worse.

"I suppose you're wondering about the, uh, the…"

"Lawsuit? Where you're suing me for abandonment?"

He flushed, put out his smoke and got another one from the crushed pack of Camels. "It's not personal," he said. "You shouldn't take it personal."

"I shouldn't? My father is suing me. The man who walked out the door all those years ago and never bothered to come back? Who didn't even leave a note for his only kid? Why shouldn't I take that personally?"

He didn't answer her or look at her. "The lawyer. He's the one that said I should do it this way. That you wouldn't care. That you had, like, insurance to deal with this kind of thing."

"I don't. If you win the lawsuit, you get money from my pocket. Money that I earned, no thanks to you."

"But you gave your mother a lot of money. I know that."

"My mother didn't leave me. My mother did her best to try and survive after you walked out."

"Well, I am your father. You can't deny that!"

"No," she said. "I can't. You are my biological father. But that's all you are to me. Just an accident of nature. I stopped liking you a long time ago. I stopped loving you two days ago.''

"But you'll still, uh, give me some…"

"Yes. I'll give you some money. Not even close to ten million, which, by the way, is laughable. My attorney will be in touch with your attorney. If you want to go ahead with the lawsuit, be my guest. But if you do, I'll appeal until it's too late. You won't see a nickel.''

"Okay, sure. That's all I'm saying. Just enough to get by. The winters can be damn cold.''

She knew what the money was going to pay for. Booze. Gambling. He'd probably use the cash to drink himself to death. But everyone made choices in life. And everyone had to live with the consequences of those choices.

"I hope it makes you happy,'' she said, standing. "I truly do.''

She left before he had a chance to say anything more. As she slipped out the front door, she realized there was nothing, absolutely nothing keeping her in Austin. She might as well pack up and go back to New York. Regroup. Figure out what she was going to do with herself.

She didn't realize she was weeping until she got into the car. And then it was too late to stop the flood of tears. It had all gone so wrong.

MITCH CLOSED his office door and leaned his forehead against the cool wood. He'd done something he'd never contemplated before—he'd canceled his whole afternoon. On a busy Monday, no less. Those who couldn't make the change were being seen by a colleague. His secretary had looked worried, but he didn't care. He didn't seem to care about much right now.

The thing was, he couldn't shake the feeling he was screwing up. Badly. The thought of losing Darcy had him running scared.

Every time he closed his eyes, she was waiting for him. He'd thought he'd seen her four times today, once while looking at his sister.

He couldn't shake her. He couldn't shake the feeling of dread. And all the while, he kept hearing Angela's voice, but he couldn't make out the words.

For a moment, he debated telling Eleanor to stop making calls, that he'd see his patients, but he didn't. The most he could seem to accomplish at the moment was to open his eyes and walk to his chair. He stared out the window, right at the tree that had grown up with him. The tree with their initials, carved for all time.

He turned toward his desk and opened the bottom drawer. At the very back, he found an envelope. It took him several minutes to open it. When he did, a single photograph fell onto his desk blotter.

Angela. Such a pretty girl. So soft, so easy. She'd never asked him for a thing. Except a child. Except for her life.

The longer he looked at her, the deeper his sadness. Such a waste. Such a tragedy. If only—

If only. Was that what he wanted his life to be about? If only he'd saved her? If only they had waited to get pregnant? If only he'd loved her like he should have? Like he loved Darcy?

Like he still loved Darcy.

He stared at the photograph as if he'd just seen it for the first time. Angela had been important to him. She'd been a good friend and a good wife. And she'd died. The child she carried had died, too. Why? Because he'd failed? Or because there was a bigger plan at work?

How many times had his mother told him that? Told him that he'd never be really happy until he forgave himself and Angela.

What would it mean if he did forgive himself? Would it mean he betrayed Angela yet again?

The face in the photograph seemed to laugh. He closed his eyes and heard her voice once more. It was a simple message. Only one word. *Goodbye.*

DARCY WRAPPED one of her new cups in paper, then put it in the box for shipping. She'd never used the cup. It had been in the cupboard for less than a week. The Pottery Barn shipment had been returned. The decorator fired.

She'd had such hopes for this house. If she closed her eyes, she could hear her unborn children on the stairs, laughing.

It wasn't fair.

Why shouldn't she have a family? Just because she'd been on the cover of some magazines? It wasn't even a fame she could be proud of. She'd had nothing to do with her bone structure or her height or her looks. She'd been given those things as a gift—or a curse.

But it was a strange world she lived in. A world where beauty meant more than goodness, where athletes and actors were given heroic status and the real heroes, the scientists, the freedom fighters, the teachers, were underpaid and underappreciated.

It wasn't fair. It wasn't right. And damn it, she loved him.

There was no use kidding herself. She was in love with Mitchell Maitland, and she had been all her life. No other man had come close. No one ever would.

So why the hell was she leaving?

She'd fought like a tiger to make her marriage to Tony work, despite the evidence that he never really loved her. Despite the way he treated her. Yet she'd fought with everything in her. Why? Because she believed in marriage. She believed in love. All her life, nothing had been more important to her than her dream of becoming a wife and mother. She'd have traded in every magazine cover, every commercial, every compliment.

It was Mitchell's fault she felt this way. Watching him and his family all those years. That's where she'd learned to hope. To wish.

What if…

What if she fought for her dreams? What if she stuck it out, waited for Mitch to see he wasn't to blame for what had happened in the past? It wasn't as if this was the only time she'd be able to have a baby, right? She could wait a year. Two years.

Wasn't it worth waiting if in the end she could have it all?

She got up, paced the kitchen, circled, opened the fridge and took out an apple. Then she sat at her new kitchen table and took a big old bite.

As she chewed, her thoughts spun a hundred miles an hour. Weighing the pros and cons, looking at the worst-case scenario, and the best. What it all came down to was the children.

She'd seen, too vividly, what happened when people who shouldn't have had children had them anyway. Her parents would have been so much wiser to forget about kids. They'd have done so much less damage.

On the other hand, here she was. Was she sorry to have been born? No. Of course not. She'd had a hell of a wonderful life despite her parents. Or who knows, maybe because of her parents.

Maybe that was the lesson. It was so easy to see how Mitch blamed himself for things he couldn't have possibly prevented, so why couldn't she see the same thing about her life? She was dealt a hand, and it was her job to make the best of the cards. Not sit around and mope because it wasn't a royal flush.

The most important thing about her was her capacity to love, and if she forgot that, she'd end up bitter and miserable like her mother. Or drunk like her father. She had a choice here.

She tossed her apple core into the sink, a surge of energy shooting through her body. She was going to fight. She was going to marry Mitchell Maitland. And they were going to have babies together. Lots of them.

Woe to the person who got in her way.

The sign. The real estate lady had left twenty minutes ago after putting the For Sale sign in the front yard. Darcy headed outside. It would feel good to rip the thing right out of the ground.

But as she touched the sign, she heard a car behind

her. The press, no doubt. But so what? Nothing and no one was going to stop her.

"Darcy!"

She whirled at the sound of the familiar voice. Mitch! He flung open the door even before the car had come to a complete stop, and he headed toward her with such determination her heart started pounding in her chest.

When he got to her, he took her arms in his hands and pulled her to him. He looked at her with fire in his gaze and then he kissed her. Kissed her silly. Kissed her sane.

"I won't let you go," he said. "I can't. I don't care what it takes. You're staying. We'll fight the lawsuit. We'll chase the press away. We'll do whatever we have to because, damn it, Darcy, you belong with me. You always have."

Darcy felt the tears come, felt her whole body shake with great, racking sobs.

"Oh, God!" Mitch held on to her, but he looked positively panicked. "What's wrong?"

She shook her head. Pointed to the sign. But she couldn't talk yet. She tried, but she couldn't.

He looked at her, looked at the sign, then he ripped the wooden flag out of the ground with a roar, threw it down and smashed it in half with his feet.

When he turned to her, he put his hands on his hips. She was glad he hadn't worn a jacket, because a jacket would have spoiled the effect.

He looked perfect. Everything about him made her happy. There was only one thing missing.

"Well?" he asked.

"Why?" she said, although it came out in kind of croak.

"Why?"

She nodded, wiping her eyes and her nose with her shirtsleeve. "Why should I stay?"

He crooked his head to the right. Gave her a stare that was pure disbelief. "Wait here," he said. "Don't move."

She nodded. He ran to his car and pulled something from the back seat. She didn't know what it was until he got close enough to touch. "The time capsule!"

He nodded. "It's time we opened it."

She wondered what this had to do with her questions, but then Mitch broke the seal on the old lunch box. She looked inside, and the first thing she saw was the ribbon from the science fair. Mitch rummaged through the memorabilia, making it hard for her to see. His hand stilled finally, and he broke into a slow smile. He showed her what he'd found. A Hallmark card she'd never seen before.

On the cover was a picture of a tree. An oak tree. She opened the card. There wasn't a preprinted message on the inside. In fact, there were just a few letters on the page.

DT+MM FOREVER

"Does that answer your question?" he asked. "I love you, Darcy. Always have. Always will."

That was it. Those were the words. She launched herself at him, and thank goodness his reflexes were good. He caught her in midair. She kissed him, a big sloppy kiss, and he kissed her, over and over. Finally, she pulled back, but only slightly. "I love you, too."

"Hey, Taylor?" he said.

''What, Maitland?''

''I don't know how you feel about it, but I want kids. Lots of kids.''

She burst into tears again. But Mitch didn't let her go. He kept holding her tight. Keeping her safe. Welcoming her home.

* * * * *

MAITLAND MATERNITY
continues with
BILLION DOLLAR BRIDE
by
Muriel Jensen

Landing the account for the Cahill-Lamont wedding had an unexpected fringe benefit, event planner Anna Maitland had to admit. Her son, Will, got to meet his idol, Austin Cahill. The problem was, the charismatic Mr. Cahill was proving pretty irresistible to Will's mom, too, even though she was doing a bang-up job of arranging his wedding to another woman!

Available next month.

Here's a preview!

CHAPTER ONE

"YOUR SON TOLD ME he wishes I was marrying you," Austin said, "instead of Caroline."

Anna didn't react at all, her face revealing nothing. "I'm sure you told Will that you've made a binding promise," she said quietly, "and that I'm not the kind of woman you're looking for."

He'd apparently underestimated her reserves of quick thinking. But a sudden tightening of the atmosphere between them and the nature of that last remark made him wonder if that wasn't her way of finding out what was on *his* mind.

"You're not?" he asked.

"I'd have to be loved," she said, folding her arms and squaring her shoulders, as though she were taking a stand. "I wasn't the first time, and I'd really like to know what that's like. And I'd want to be loved for me, not just for my ability to reproduce."

Okay. She had him there. She'd have to be loved, and he just wasn't into that anymore. It was more than a fear of being hurt again, it was a reluctance to be that vulnerable.

He grinned. "Then maybe you'd just let me adopt Will."

Laughter bubbled out of her, then she looked sad—

almost as though she regretted his admission that she wasn't the type of woman he was looking for.

"The Fair Trade Commission probably wouldn't allow it," she said. "The two of you could probably rule the world."

Then without warning—probably because she hadn't even know herself that she was going to touch him—she put her hand to his sleeve. "Thank you for dinner. Will had such a good...time."

A charge went straight to his heart, as though she'd used defibrillation paddles on him.

He saw her eyes widen and guessed that the charge had kicked back.

She dropped her hand instantly, looked first disoriented and then angry, then turned to go.

He caught her hand, the charge ricocheting inside his body. He didn't understand it but couldn't figure it. He pulled her toward him.

The anger was gone from her eyes and she just looked sad. "Austin, don't even think about it!" she whispered.

"I'm not thinking," he said, still pulling. "I'm just doing."

The night was cool, the air crisp and redolent of pine and the promise of spring. The wind sighed and the leaves whispered, and something shouted inside him. "Don't—let—her—go!"

She let him draw her into his arms until they were body to body and he could see himself reflected in her eyes. Her upturned face was pale and perfectly sculpted, and her bottom lip gave one betraying quiver.

Then she firmed it and wedged a space between them with her hands against his chest.

"You're engaged," she reminded him quietly.

"Can you admit to me," he asked, "that there's something here?"

Her eyes met his honestly, filled with whatever that something was. It couldn't be love, could it, if he couldn't give it and she wouldn't let him if he could?

"It would be foolish to deny it, wouldn't it?" she asked finally. "But that doesn't mean anything."

It shouldn't, but it did. "I can't explain it," he said, "but though it can't change the situation, it means everything to *me*."

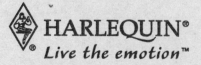

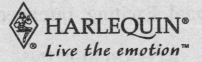

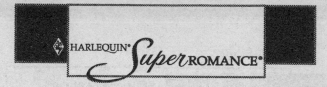

...there's more to the story!

Superromance.
A *big* satisfying read about unforgettable characters. Each month we offer *six* very different stories that range from family drama to adventure and mystery, from highly emotional stories to romantic comedies—and much more! Stories about people you'll believe in and care about. Stories too compelling to put down....

Our authors are among today's *best* romance writers. You'll find familiar names and talented newcomers. Many of them are award winners—and you'll see why!

If you want the biggest and best in romance fiction, you'll get it from Superromance!

Emotional, Exciting, Unexpected...

Live the emotion™

Harlequin Historicals®
Historical Romantic Adventure!

From rugged lawmen and valiant knights to defiant heiresses and spirited frontierswomen, Harlequin Historicals will capture your imagination with their dramatic scope, passion and adventure.

*Harlequin Historicals...
they're too good to miss!*

HARLEQUIN®
Presents®

The world's bestselling romance series...
The series that brings you your favorite authors,
month after month:

Helen Bianchin...Emma Darcy
Lynne Graham...Penny Jordan
Miranda Lee...Sandra Marton
Anne Mather...Carole Mortimer
Susan Napier...Michelle Reid

and many more uniquely talented authors!

Wealthy, powerful, gorgeous men...
Women who have feelings just like your own...
The stories you love, set in exotic, glamorous locations...

HARLEQUIN®
Presents®

Seduction and Passion Guaranteed!